The Vanished

Celia Rees

■SCHOLASTIC

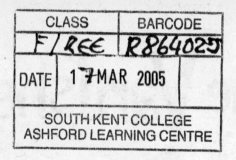

Scholastic Children's Books,
Commonwealth House, 1–19 New Oxford Street,
London, WC1A 1NU, UK
A division of Scholastic Ltd
London ~ New York ~ Toronto ~ Sydney ~ Auckland
Mexico City ~ New Delhi ~ Hong Kong

First published in the UK by Scholastic Ltd, 1997
This edition published by Scholastic Ltd, 2003

ISBN 0 439 98232 4

Printed and bound by Nørhaven Paperback, Viborg, Denmark

4 5 6 7 8 9 10

*For all my Coventry students,
in thanks for the stories they told*

1

Tunnels and culverts, storm drains and mine workings, caves and quarries, underground entrances of every kind, opening like jaws. One after another he pinned the photographs on to the board. "Danger" and "Keep Out" signs swung above black gaps in the ground, the only indication of open shafts dropping hundreds of feet down. Flotsam and jetsam – a white plastic bag, an item of clothing, a child's toy bloated and bleached by long immersion – caught like fragments of food in iron-spiked maws. Now they had been caught by the camera, hanging for ever above the oily flow of the black river water.

Jake Saunders pushed his glasses up his nose and then moved the shot of a vast concrete pipe and put it next to the tunnel which took the run off from the Brideswell Pool. The squat archway, old and stone built, had always reminded him of Traitors' Gate on the River Thames. He particularly valued that one. He had nearly fallen into the lake trying to get it, his foot slipping into the dark grey water. For a moment, back then, with licks of white mist curling around him, it felt as if something was actually pulling him... He shook his head now, dismissing it. He'd just been in danger of making a prat of himself in front of the early morning fisherman.

Jake stood back to survey his work, skinny arms folded. They were excellent photographs. He had done a brilliant job. Except he had no idea why he had taken them.

"They really are good."

He turned to the voice behind him. It was Cassie Johnson. She was a year older than him, in the sixth form, and very pretty: tall and slim, blonde hair cropped short. She was editor of the school newspaper. He looked away from the blue eyes smiling into his and felt himself blushing, uncertain whether it was because of her praise or her close proximity.

"Thanks," he replied, modest as ever, but his talent was not at issue.

"I thought you were on exam leave," she said, leaning past him for a closer look. "What are you doing here?"

"Came in to print these."

"When did you take them?"

"Early Sunday morning. Just after dawn."

She nodded. That would account for the wisps of mist and eerie pearly light. They were fascinating studies, sinister and beautiful at the same time. He had that ability, to find something extra in the mundane and ordinary.

"Nice colour effects."

Cassie pointed to the biggest tunnel. A splash of bright

pink stood out against matt black and shiny dark green. She leaned in closer. It looked as though a cardigan, or something, had got caught in the teeth of a wide open, slime-bearded mouth, twice as tall as a man.

"I'm thinking of calling them 'Underworlds'. What do you think?"

"Yeah. Good title."

If you looked at them long enough you could think an underworld, a series of them even, really did exist.

"I want to do some research based around them. Maybe work them up for an exhibition. What do you reckon?"

"Umm, interesting." Cassie nodded. Jake's projects were often ambitious and weird, a little off the wall, but he certainly had good ideas. "What made you think of it?"

Jake put his hands up, a "search me" gesture.

"Just woke up, grabbed the camera, and off I went. Must have had a dream, or something."

"Must have been some dream to make you bike it all over the city." Cassie looked at him, curious. "What was it about?"

"I don't remember." He shook his head as if the last rag of it was leaving him. "I don't think it was a good one, though."

"Umm. No."

Cassie found it hard to disagree. You could almost smell the river water, the musty decay of enclosed spaces.

"Since you're in," she said, looking at her watch, "do you think you can make the editorial meeting? My office, twelve o'clock?"

Jake nodded absently, his attention straying back to the images in front of him.

Cassie still had a million things to do, and the bell was due to go any minute, but she paused for a moment, drawn back, like him, to the photographs. Looked at together, the pictures created a sense of powerful menace, hinting at hidden spaces, *dangerous* places, just beneath the surface of things. What kind of dream could that have been?

2

Across town, Aleister Fraser was waking up from a different dream, a dream he did remember. He'd had it so many times, it felt as though it was etched inside his skull. Fraser wiped the sweat from his body with the sheet and sank back, wondering whether to get up and go to school. No one would notice if he didn't. Dad would have left already and Mum would be back asleep by now. She couldn't care less one way or the other and he wouldn't know. The school wouldn't notice. Not for a while, anyway. A day, a week, what was the difference? It might be a month, even, before they caught up with him, and by then it would be the holidays. He was new to the school, new to the area. Today was supposed to be his first day.

If he didn't go now, he might never get round to it. He sat up, pulled on black jeans and a black T-shirt and laced his boots. He ran his fingers through his long dark hair and picked up a black coat off the floor. He could not recall if the school had one, but this was his uniform.

He ripped open a pint of milk, drinking straight from the carton, and flicked the TV on to check the time. It was the local news. A little kid had gone missing. Fraser took the carton from his mouth and wiped away his white moustache. Shots of river water, cops in blue overalls walking across a scrubby common.

"Six-year-old Wendy Richardson, missing since Saturday afternoon, was last seen playing in this area…"

A path entered woodland, the vegetation forming a green tunnel, curling around itself.

"Wendy is described as being tall for her age, with blue eyes and long fair hair reaching to her waist. She was wearing white trainers, lime-green leggings, and a yellow T-shirt under a pink cardigan. Anyone who thinks they might have seen her, or has information as to her whereabouts, should contact the police on…"

The contact number appeared across the bottom of the screen, then more police and Wendy's parents talking at a press conference. Fraser put down the pint. The pain on the anguished faces was clenching his stomach, curdling the milk. He turned away from them and switched off the set.

The school was kind of gothic-looking, he did remember that. Perched up on a hill, like in "Psycho", there was more than a touch of the Amityville haunted house about it. That was one of the reasons he had chosen it. All the other schools were so boring, '60s glass and faded panelling. Campbell Roberts School looked different, at least. A wide drive curved away from the sign and Fraser started up it. The main building had been bequeathed to the city by some industrialist or other; they had told him and his dad on their preliminary visit. Behind the late-Victorian house, the school was much like any other, but the façade was impressive and the facilities were excellent. All kinds of things: computers, media, photography. He wanted to be a journalist, so all that was attractive. They also had a very good outdoor pursuits department, but that brought on that sickening, tightening feeling in his stomach. His breath became shallow and he made himself stop and regulate it like he'd been told to. *Think about what you are going to do now. This moment.* Fraser went up the wide stone steps and knocked on the big front door. *You must not think about that.*

"Pupils should not use the main entrance."

A woman looked down at him, peering over gold-rimmed half-glasses, gathering her beige cardigan close around her. Her frown deepened and her mouth pursed tighter as she took in the scruffy individual standing in front of her. Hair down to his shoulders, and a long black overcoat – in this weather! And another thing, if they were old enough to shave, they ought to make sure they did. Every morning.

"Sorry. I didn't know. I'm new." Under her scrutiny, Fraser's hand strayed to his face, rubbing at the jawline stubble. "I'm supposed to start today."

"You're two hours late. School starts at half-past eight."

"I know, I'm sorry. Couldn't get it together this morning. Well, aren't you going to let me in?"

He smiled, dark brows rising in mock-solemn enquiry, slanting green eyes darted amusement above cheekbones like knives. The effect was most disarming.

Mrs Weatherall, the school secretary, felt her own features softening.

"Of course. Come this way."

She led him into the reception area and even found herself offering him a cup of coffee. He smiled his thanks and sat, long legs sprawled, while she got on with the paper work. The girls in the office on work experience couldn't stop staring at him. Even she couldn't help sneaking a glance in his direction. He really was rather a handsome boy.

Fraser sat on a low leather chair, waiting to be processed. He looked round, studying his surroundings bit by bit. Inside, the spooky-house feel intensified. The foyer was big, shadowy and quiet. The black and white marble tiles beneath his feet were set out in an odd, intricate design, winding round and round like a labyrinth. High ceilings swallowed the keyboard chatter and dark, oak panelling deadened the noise from outside. The kids' playtime shouting sounded far away and unreal, like bird cries. A huge mahogany staircase led away to darkened landings, unknown upper storeys. A fierce looking old geezer, with a ferocious expression and lots of white whiskers, frowned down from a big, gloomy oil painting set high up on the far wall. *Lt. Col. William Campbell Roberts*, it said underneath in half-rubbed out gold leaf. He must have lived here once. Fraser wondered what he'd think if he came back now.

"That is a portrait of Colonel Campbell Roberts."

"Excuse me?"

That woman, the secretary, was talking to him again.

"The father of Frederick Campbell Roberts. The man who gave this house to the city."

"Oh, right."

"This was the library, in their day. The deputy head should be able to see you now." She put her hand on the phone. "I'll just see if she is free."

More waiting. Fraser fidgeted for a while and then stood up and wandered about. He found sitting still difficult. A notice board ran the length of the wall by the door that led into the main part of the school. Fraser walked from one end to the other reading the notices about play rehearsals and cricket fixtures. Somewhere past the middle he stopped. One particular notice caught his attention. He went back to read it again.

ORBIT MEETING
MONDAY 12:00 IN THE *ORBIT* OFFICE
ANYONE OUT THERE INTERESTED?
WE MEAN YOU!
PLEASE COME!

"What's this *Orbit* thing?" he asked, going over to the secretary.

"It's the school newspaper. Comes out once a fortnight."

"Where's this meeting?"

"They have an office. Top of the House."

He looked round, mystified.

"Where's that?"

"Here. This part of the school is always referred to as the House."

"Oh, right."

"Interested?"

He looked back at the notice.

"Might be."

"Good," she smiled up at him. "The school likes people who get stuck in. Be sure and mention it to the deputy head. She'll see you now."

Fraser's interview with the deputy head went on longer than he expected. She had the report from his last school in front of her and had obviously read it carefully. She insisted he go over the whole thing again. Her interest and concern took up lots of time and now he was late. He ran up the last narrow flight of stairs. The *Orbit* office was right at the top. When he finally arrived, there was some kind of row going on. It was so intense that they didn't even notice him. He stood leaning against the door-jamb for a while, just watching.

A good-looking blonde girl in jeans and a white T-shirt was sitting in front of a computer console. She seemed to be in charge, but she was sitting back in her chair right now, hands in pockets, being harangued by a chubby girl in a suit. Two lads were lounging about and scowling. One was big; broad shoulders straining his check shirt. The other was thinner with long, lank mousy hair tied back in a ponytail. A geeky-looking younger kid, ginger crew-cut and glasses, leant against a filing cabinet, arms folded. They were all listening. The big girl in the tight suit seemed to be calling the shots.

"Bottom line is, if sales don't improve we will be withdrawing funding."

The two lads let out howls of indignation.

"Stop power-tripping, Louise," the bigger of the two boys snarled. "It's just a stupid Business Enterprise Scheme. It's not real money."

"We have designated funds," Louise was going red and beginning to tremble, "and as business manager…"

"Stuff it, Louise," Ponytail sneered.

"Yeah. Go suck on a shoulder pad."

The two lads cracked up at this and Louise reached for her asthma inhaler.

The blonde girl used the gap to intervene.

"Louise is right." She ran her fingers through her short hair. "We can't even give papers away. And no wonder. Who's going to buy a paper with no stories?"

"It ain't our fault," Check shirt offered.

"Not entirely," his thin mate added.

"Whose is it, then?" Their editor's voice had gone dangerously quiet. She clicked on the screen in front of her, scrolling up empty pages. "Your contribution so far for this week's edition. Precisely zilch. Why do I always end up doing everything myself?"

"It's out of season."

"Not much going on."

"Did it ever occur to you that there are other sports besides football?"

"Like what?" the two lads demanded in unison. It seemed this was a revelation.

"Like cricket, tennis, athletics?" The blonde girl counted them off on her fingers.

The two boys looked at each other.

"But they're all boring!" they said together.

"OK." The editor sighed and clicked on to another blank inside page. "What about all these riveting interviews with local bands? What about the gig guide?"

"They split up."

"Half the gigs were cancelled."

There was a pause. The blonde girl regarded the two of them with such deep contempt, Fraser felt like applauding.

"We could do some reviews, I suppose," Check shirt offered sulkily.

"Fine," she hissed through gritted teeth. "That's settled, then. So go away and do it!"

"Hi." Fraser judged this a good point to introduce himself. "I've come for the *Orbit* meeting. Have I got the right place? My name's Fraser."

"Oh, hello." The blonde girl looked up at him, her blue eyes widening. "Yes, you've got the right place. I'm Cassie, I'm the editor. This is Louise, our, ahem, business manager." The big girl simpered and straightened her skirt. "This is Jake, our photographer." The ginger-headed boy nodded and pushed his glasses up his nose. "And, er, Todd and Warren – our reporters." The latter two regarded him with undisguised hostility, doubly put off by his general appearance and his clipped, precise way of speaking. "You're welcome," she added with a sigh. "Anyone is."

Louise stood up, using his entrance as her cue to leave for another "meeting".

"I can't stand her," Todd said, as soon as she was out of the room.

"Fat moose!" Warren added, loud enough for her to hear.

"It's not her fault." Cassie held up a hand to quell the outburst.

"What's the problem?" Fraser asked, going over to the window. It was tall and barred, looking down on to a courtyard many feet below.

"Circulation. It has reached what Louise terms a 'critical low'."

"That's easy to solve."

"How's that?"

"Well, it worked like a dream at my old school and this one has much more potential."

"For what?"

"Spooking it up."

"How do you mean?"

"The Unexplained." He grinned. "Mystery Incidents – kids love it!"

"Like what?"

Fraser shrugged. "Like – anything that happens."

"What if nothing does?"

"It always does. School this size, there's always something going on. Accidents happen every day. What matters is the way you report it."

"Like how?"

"OK. Say you drop all your files and papers down the stairs."

"Where's the story in that?"

"There isn't one. But say an unseen hand pushed you, jogged your elbow, then a cold draft from nowhere scattered the papers down the stairs. Say it had happened before, and always at that point…"

"Yeah!" Warren, the lad in the check shirt, grinned. "And say next time it's a kid, not a file."

"Or maybe there *was* a kid," Todd joined in, "fell down the stairs and killed himself. Come to think of it," he paused, his brow creased in thought, "I reckon something like that *did* happen…"

Fraser smiled. "Now you're getting my drift."

"I still don't see…"

"I do." Jake spoke for the first time. "I think it's a good idea. I like it. It's better than those two and their rubbish bands and hopeless football teams."

"Hey!" Warren objected. "Now just hang on a minute…" He glared at Jake, fists balled, but the ginger-headed boy stared calmly back. He was tougher than he looked. He was excellent at outdoor pursuits, a fearless climber and intrepid caver, and was going for his Duke of Edinburgh Gold Award next year. He was not scared by much, certainly not by the likes of Warren and Todd.

"Let's vote." Cassie wasn't sure about this, but she was keen to avert further argument. "All in favour of Fraser's idea?" She glanced round. "Unanimous."

Across the courtyard, the big plate glass windows reflected the summer sun like a wall of mirrors. Then one slowly began to disintegrate. There was no crash, no smashing sound – it simply began to fall. They all looked out, alerted by the sudden difference in the light, and watched the sections of glass descend as if in slow motion, to break into a million pieces, shattering over the cars parked in the yard.

"There you are!" Fraser turned to them, green eyes glittering like the splintering shards. "If I'm not mistaken, you have your first story."

3

It went exactly as Fraser predicted. Various minor
incidents and accidents that occurred during the
school week were transformed into *Orbit*'s first
"Stranger than Fiction" edition.

Friday was deadline day and all the copy was in. This
was a minor miracle in itself, Cassie reflected as she
checked the front page. The stories were running under
the banner headline: *School Hit by Outbreak of Mystery
Events!*

Underneath, the page broke down into individual
stories: *Mystery Fire in Science Lab* by Todd Dover,
reported a fire which had broken out in Science 2. Not
that this was news to anyone; the alarms had gone off
and the whole school had been evacuated to stand on the
field for nearly an hour waiting for the fire service to
give the all clear. Very little real damage had been done
but, as Todd reported, the lab had been locked, hadn't
been used since the day before.

So what was the cause? Was this a case of spontaneous combustion? Unexplained forces making things burst into flame for no apparent reason. Or was it telekinesis? The ability to start fires by mind power *alone? Was there a* fire starter *at work within the school community? Where would he (or she) strike next?*

It was a good piece. Todd had written more, and better, than he had for ages. It even looked like he'd been to the library. Cassie could feel the pull of the story, the sense of mystery and strangeness. After all, even if you ignored the stuff about spontaneous combustion and telwhatsit, as she did, obviously, you could not dismiss the basic facts. The fire had occurred in a locked laboratory, and the way it started had not been satisfactorily explained.

She went on to the lead story: *White Mist Brings on Near Fatal Attack – Sixth-former Tells of Strange Experience* by A L Fraser.

Cassie wondered what the A L stood for; so far she had only known him as Fraser. She found herself thinking about him far too much lately. She forced herself back to reading the story.

Sixth-former and Young Enterprise Business Manager, Louise Kennedy, describes her terrifying experience... Cassie knew all about this incident. It had been pretty scary at the time, and dramatic; Louise herself had made sure of that. Mustn't be bitchy, she reminded herself, as she edited out the Business Manager title.

Louise had been walking along the upper corridor in the House – just after having been to see Cassie as a matter of fact – when she had seen a strange white mist creeping towards her along the floor. She had also been aware of a sudden drop in temperature. She had stood, transfixed, staring at the white mist, when all of a sudden it had seemed to her as if there were figures, *ghostly* figures, walking through it towards her, as thin and insubstantial as the mist itself. This had been too much for Louise. The shock and fear had brought on a serious asthma attack. She had groped in her bag for her inhaler, but in her panic, could not find it, although she was absolutely positive that she had put it in the front pocket.

Fraser had found her on her knees, hyperventilating. Apparently he was a fellow sufferer, another thing Cassie did not know about him, and had known what to do. He had taken immediate action to regulate her breathing and then located her inhaler and helped her to apply it. Louise reckoned he had saved her life, which Cassie doubted, but he had certainly saved her from a trip to sick bay, even hospital. Louise had been gushing in her praise for him. She'd been following him around like a puppy ever since. "Is Fraser here? We were going to work on my story..." Cassie parodied the other girl's slightly lisping voice to herself. He couldn't fancy Louise, surely? Cassie shook her head, surprised at the direction her thoughts were taking. Could this be jealousy creeping in? She forced her attention back to her copy-editing.

No one else witnessed this incident but it made a good story. Whatever had happened to bring on such a severe attack must have been pretty frightening. Fraser had dug up a story from one of the cleaners about a couple of similar incidents involving white mists and mystery figures occurring on that corridor. They went back, and here comes the punchline, to a time when a child, a member of the original Campbell Roberts family, had disappeared.

There was one other small story, linking an outbreak of petty vandalism to poltergeist activity, but that had been cut on Fraser's advice. There was no need to overdo it in the first issue. Cassie looked at her watch. It was past four, she needed to get this down to printing. Where was Jake with the pictures? Maybe he'd had to go and pick up his kid sister from the junior school next door, as he did sometimes if his mum couldn't make it. Deadline days made Cassie tense and jumpy. She leaned back, trying to relax, telling herself that, of all of them, he was the most reliable. "If I say I'll be there, I'll be there," he said, and that was almost always true.

She turned to the two inner pages of the four-page paper. This was Fraser's responsibility and, she had to say, he'd made a good job of it. He had split the regular columns up into interlocking boxes, using parts of the program she hadn't even known existed; it looked like a spread in a regular teen magazine. He had called it the Psi Files.

Cassie was not entirely convinced by the title, but had been overruled by Todd and Warren. The "P" was silent, Fraser had explained; "Psi" was pronounced "si". Strictly, "psi" stood for psychic powers, extrasensory perception, but Fraser reckoned it would do for anything weird, un-explained, paranormal. Todd and Warren thought it was a cool idea, "like those two on the telly". They had been so impressed they had even volunteered to do work for it – another first – finding information to fill the little boxes

that made up the page. These contained facts and defini-
tions of different phenomenon and little snippets: strange-
but-true anecdotes. In the middle was a Kitchener figure,
with his finger pointing out at the reader, saying:

YOUR PAPER NEEDS YOU!
Send us YOUR stories!
We'll publish the best in our
regular readers' feature.
ANYTHING WEIRD WILL DO!

"Now what do you reckon to that? Brilliant, or
what?"

Cassie turned to see Fraser's vivid green eyes gazing
down into hers.

"We'll see," she commented noncommittally,
swinging her chair back and away from him, discon-
certed to find him suddenly so near to her, disturbed by
the way he was making her feel.

Fraser stood behind her, arms folded.

"I'm telling you, it's a winner. Kids love to read this kind
of stuff, especially if it's local, or happened to someone they
know, and everyone knows someone something has
happened to. The stories'll come in by the sackful. And –
this is the really good bit – everyone who sends in a story
buys a paper to see if they are in it. Guaranteed sales!" He
spread his long arms wide as if to embrace his own
cleverness. "It *cannot* fail!"

"I'll tell you one thing," Cassie replied, clicking on
"save", "we won't sell anything if we don't get this in for
printing and I can't take it down until Jake scans in the
pictures…"

As if on cue, the skinny ginger-headed photographer ambled in through the door.

"Had to fetch Amy and she had a music lesson. Sorry I'm late."

Jake was followed in by his kid sister, carrying her clarinet case. She knew everyone there except Fraser. She stopped in front of him, smiling uncertainly.

"Hi, my name's Fraser," he said, looking down at her.

She was about eight and pretty, with delicate features. The looks in the Saunders family must have skipped her brother and landed on her. His mass of freckles thinned to a charming few, spread evenly across her creamy cheeks and little upturned nose as though dotted on by a paint brush. His vibrant hair had been soothed to silky strawberry-blonde curls and, although they shared the same blue eyes, hers were large and wide, unobscured by glasses.

"Hello," she replied. "My name's Amy."

Fraser shook the solemnly offered small hand and smiled for a moment.

"Pleased to meet you," he said quickly, and then abruptly turned away.

He went over to the other desk to join Todd and Warren. There was something he couldn't bear about her candid little-kid gaze and the look of pride and love on her big brother's face.

Jake stayed to file his negatives while Amy accompanied Cassie down to the print room.

Todd laughed at something Fraser said, and Warren commented, "She never goes out with kids from school. She's unpullable."

Jake bent his head over the filing cabinet. He knew who they were talking about, and what they were talking about, and it made his blood boil.

Todd laughed again. "You got no chance, mate."

"Want to bet?" Fraser said, his clipped voice soft and challenging.

"Sure," Todd replied. "How about a tenner?"

"Tenner's fine," Fraser agreed. "How about you?"

"Yeah, I'm in," Warren replied.

"We have a bet then, gentlemen," Fraser said, and Jake heard the rustle of paper money and skin slap on skin. "A tenner says I do."

Jake rammed the top filing-cabinet drawer home and wrenched the next one open. They were older than him, and there were three of them, but he felt like going over there and ripping them limb from limb. How could they talk that way about Cassie?

"Cassie, Cassie! Wait up. Wait for me!" Fraser loped out of school after her, catching her easily as she walked down the long drive. "I was kind of wondering," he said as he fell into step beside her, "I mean, I'm new round here, I don't know anyone except you, and I don't know where to go or what to do, so…"

"So?"

"So I was wondering if, I mean, if you haven't got anything on, that is, I was wondering if you would go out with me this evening?"

Cassie stopped dead in her tracks. She was not sure what she was expecting, but it was not that. She looked up at him, ready to refuse, but he looked so genuinely bashful she took pity on him.

"OK."

"What?" He stood, confused. He had not expected her consent.

"I said, OK. Yes. I will go out with you."

"Great! I'll pick you up about eight." He ran on, but halfway down the path, he turned and trotted back. "Where do you live?"

She laughed and took a sheet of paper from her file.

"Are you sure you'll find it?" she asked.

Todd and Warren walked past, wheeling their bikes. Cassie was too busy writing her address to see Fraser's thumbs-up.

"Oh, I'll find it all right," he said, taking the paper from her hand. "No problem."

He waved and ran on again, leaving Cassie to continue alone. The long winding drive was bordered on either side by dense overhanging shrubbery. Huge rhododendron bushes, their big flowers browning and dying now, spread their leathery leaves, filling the spaces between towering trees. Even on the brightest day, the tangled foliage shaded away light into darkness.

Cassie walked on, lost in her own thoughts, unaware of a figure, a white face keeping pace with her, dodging in and out of the interlocking branches. He made no noise, and she did not see him until he darted out in front of her. She nearly fell over him, but he eluded her steadying hand, veering off like some hunted animal, leaving her with the fleeting impression of a face hazed with dirt, drained of any colour. His clothes were black, threadbare; his sneakers cracked and caked with mud. He looked poor, undernourished. She half-expected him to ask if she could spare some change before he disappeared into the other side of the shrubbery. She had seen him around, she thought he went to the school, but he was just another face from the ever-changing mêlée of the playground.

She shook her head, dismissing him, and her mind turned to other things. She felt good. The idea for the paper was going to work. It could turn it round, make it a success. Going out on a date would be a good way to celebrate. She hugged her file to her, resting her chin on it, suddenly not sure if going out with Fraser was a sensible idea. After all, she knew nothing about him. On the other hand, she smiled to herself, he was handsome, and new, and different from the other boys. Sensible or not, that made for a pretty exciting prospect.

She left the school gates and turned towards home. The boy watched her from a vantage point twenty feet above. He sat in the fork of a tree, so motionless he seemed part of it. Cassie didn't know who he was, but lots of the younger kids did. Even Amy could have told her; he appeared in their playground, too. Cassie didn't know his name now, but soon she would. His name was Billy.

4

Cassie didn't think about Billy again, not for the whole weekend, although he was here and there, around and about, hanging out in the streets, down the precinct, but Cassie failed to notice. Billy was careful to be invisible to her, and anyway, she was busy with Fraser.

Friday night he took her out for a meal and then a drink after that. On Saturday Cassie offered to show him the tourist spots and then they went round the shops. When he took her home, her mum invited him in, and he stayed for supper.

Cassie could not remember the last time she enjoyed being with someone so much. He was charming, (her mother melted instantly), and funny, (he kept Cassie laughing the whole weekend), but he could be serious as well. He had a keen intelligence and wide knowledge, talking endlessly about anything and everything. Everything, that is, except himself.

By Sunday, Cassie realized he knew just about

everything there was to know about her, from childhood injuries down to the toys she used to play with and the names of her junior-school teachers. He had met her family, talked to her mum and dad, played football with her brothers, even chatted up her older sister home from university, but Cassie still knew next to nothing about him. She knew his first name was Aleister but no one ever called him by it, and that he had spent time in Scotland which accounted for his accent, but how long? And where had he lived before that? These kind of questions were met with a shrug of the shoulders and "just different places". She did not know when exactly he had moved here, or whether his family intended to stay, or even where he was living.

"On one of the new estates," he answered vaguely when she asked him.

His dad was, "in computers", but what he did, or for which company, was answered with another shrug of the shoulders.

His mother stayed home. Doing what? He shook his head, and said "How should I know?" She didn't feed him, that was obvious. Cassie had never seen anyone eat so much. His appetite at Saturday's supper brought an invitation to Sunday lunch; Cassie's mother liked a boy who enjoyed his food. So he spent Sunday afternoon wolfing down barbecue and playing in the garden with Sean and Daniel, her nine-year-old twin brothers.

He was so popular with them, Cassie had to ask her mum to stop them pestering. They were plaguing him to exhaustion.

"Have you got any brothers or sisters?" she asked, when they were eventually left alone.

"No."

"It's just, you seem to get on so well…"

"I'm an only child. No siblings of any kind. All right?"
His abrupt reply left Cassie floundering.

"Yes, fine." She sat back in her garden chair, noting the sudden plunge in temperature. By now she was beginning to be able to read the *back off, don't ask* signs.

"Sorry," he said. "I didn't mean to be like that. It's just…" He gazed off towards the shouting twins; they were climbing trees now and arguing. He watched them for a while, an expression very like pain clouding his eyes and quirking his forehead. "It's just," he said with a sigh, "I'm not used to anyone trying to get close…"

"I didn't mean to pry."

"It's not you, it's me. You have to give me time, that's all." He finished his beer and stood up. "I've got to go. Say thanks to your mum for me."

He was a hit with the family. Even Jill, her older sister, pronounced him, "a whole lot better than the usual dorks you go out with", but there were things Cassie herself was less than sure about. It wasn't that she didn't like him because she certainly did, almost too much, that was part of the trouble. It wasn't the man-of-mystery act. He had a right to keep his past private, she could respect that. It was other things, small things. For example, something was going on with Todd and Warren. Those two had been in the pub on Friday night, and they kept looking over, nudging each other, and one of them had given Fraser a thumbs-up sign.

"They're just a couple of prats," he'd said when she'd asked him about it.

Cassie didn't disagree with that, but when Fraser went

to the bar to get more drinks, he was laughing with them and joking. The three of them seemed to be getting on just fine. Maybe they were talking about football, or some other boy thing. Maybe she was worrying about nothing. Although she had two brothers, boys of all ages remained a mystery to her.

The other thing that disturbed her was to do with the school newspaper. On Saturday, when he came back to her house, Cassie showed him a finished copy. It was something he said then that set the alarm bells ringing.

Fraser nodded his approval of the front page and Cassie had to agree, it really did look a winner. It was different from anything else they had ever done. The headlines grabbed immediate attention and Jake's photography made even Science 2 look creepy. As for the top corridor – the scene of Louise's brush with unknown forces – Cassie doubted whether anyone below year ten would ever go up there again. She was pleased, no doubt about it, but that did not stop her from thinking about how they were going to follow it.

"Simple. Once the stories from the kids start rolling in," Fraser stared down at the paper, arms folded, "they more or less write it for you."

"Yeah, but what about before then? I mean," she spread her hands, "the fire in the science lab, Louise's asthma attack, they make good stories, but how do we know anything else like that is going to happen? We can't guarantee it."

Fraser looked up, giving her that strange half-smile again. Then he rubbed his chin thoughtfully, green eyes glinting.

"Want to bet?"

5

Word on the new-look *Orbit* and the "Stranger than Fiction" edition spread through the school like wild fire. By Monday lunchtime the first run was sold out. Cassie spent her free period in the afternoon doing another one, but these copies went almost immediately, too. They even had kids queuing up outside the office asking for them. *Orbit*s were changing hands in classroom and playground for double the marked price and, by four o'clock, they had sold more papers in one day than they had in the whole of the past three-month period.

Cassie was well pleased, but like any good editor, she only allowed herself about five minutes satisfaction before she began to worry about filling the next edition.

She needn't have been concerned. Unexplained phenomena began occurring thick and fast. First, the school bell which marked the beginning and end of lessons went haywire, going off at all times of the day and throughout the night. The school got the electricians in, but no sooner had they fixed it, than the whole thing started up again. The bell had to be switched off altogether in the end. Kids were sent round with a hand bell which, of course, not everybody heard, causing even more chaos.

Just when they reckoned that was sorted, all the computers crashed: admin, library, computer rooms, everything. Only the *Orbit* office was excluded, because it was not on a network and used a completely different system. This caused a serious panic, all the school's records were in jeopardy. Computer-maintenance engineers, brought in from outside, stood around shaking their heads, looking grim. They diagnosed a virus, but just as they were about to give it all up for lost, the system started up again. The interference was only temporary; the virus was programmed to self-destruct.

Electronic interference was not the only thing happening. A couple of classrooms had been trashed, a set of lockers turned over, a shelf full of used crockery and cutlery had crashed to the floor in the dining hall nearly causing a communal heart-attack.

Something new was happening every day. No, more often than that. By the end of the week it seemed like every hour brought in news of fresh mayhem from some place or other. School life had never been this rich or this varied. The Head was on the rampage about it, and he was not looking for supernatural causes.

"He can rampage all he likes," Todd said, as he stared into the word-processor. He was in the *Orbit* office working through lunchtime on his story: "School Suffers Outbreak of Poltergeist Phenomena". "No one's put their hand up for anything, and, if you ask me, they ain't likely to. I mean," he added, warming to his theme, "take them lockers, they went over in lesson time, no one near them, duty monitor didn't see no one. Same with the classrooms. Locked before. Locked after." He winked. "Weird, or what?"

"Yeah, right." Warren grinned agreement. "It has to be a poltergeist. Let's hope the punters think so, even if it's not."

"What do you mean?" Cassie enquired from her desk, alerted by something in his tone. "Even if it's not?"

"Nothing." Warren rubbed at his scrubby fair hair.

Cassie's eyes narrowed. "If it's not poltergeist activity, what could it be?"

"Nothing. You tell me," Warren said, evasively. He stole a look at Todd before going back to his work without another word.

Cassie stood up and stretched. "How are you getting on, anyway?" she asked, coming over to his desk.

"All right," Warren said, without looking up.

Warren was helping with the Anything Weird Will Do section. The response from readers had exceeded even Fraser's expectations. There were piles and piles of readers' stories, varying from a few scrawled lines to full-length essays. Some of the English staff had picked up on it as a fun end-of-termish thing to write about and whole class contributions had now been added to the volume.

"You need to sort them out into sections," Cassie advised, marking the categories off on her fingers. "Obvious copies from other stories, like Stephen King and horror movies, ones that are too silly, too fantastic, or too gory, and ones of genuine interest."

Warren put down the paper he was reading and stared up at her, a pained expression creasing his broad face.

"Oh, really? You aren't the only one with a brain, you know. What do you think I'm doing, Cass?"

"OK, OK. I was only trying to help."

Cassie shrugged and leaned over his shoulder, picking up a story at random. She glanced through the contents for a moment, and then groaned.

"Oh, no. Have you seen this one? I knew this would happen. Listen. 'Me and my mates were camping out in a field behind our house,'" she read. "'There was a bunch of us from the estate and we were all telling stories, to scare each other. One kid tells this one about a race of vampire children...'" Cassie laughed out loud, "Vampire children, can you believe it? 'They live right here,'" she read on, "'under the city and come out at night to prey on people. Usually little kids, but they ain't fussy, sometimes they take big ones, too. They got little red eyes that glow in the dark and feet like rats. Their nails are long, all black and twisted, grown into claws. Their teeth are pointed, sharp like steel, and they use these to suck your blood. They were regular kids once, but something happened to them.

"'It don't sound so scary now, writing it down, but it was then, in that field in the middle of the night, some of us was bricking it. Then there was this knock, more a kind of bulge really, on the tent flap, and the zip started to go up. We all jumped a mile, even some of the bigger lads. It was this kid none of us had ever seen before. He wanted a light, that was all, but I swear his eyes sparked red in the flame from the lighter and the hand curling round his fag looked like it had claws on. I was of out there, I can tell you. I went back home, soon as he had gone, and slept in my own bed that night. With the light on.'

"Vampire children!" Cassie laughed again, waving the paper in front of her. "I mean, honestly! Which one is your rubbish pile?"

Warren took the story from her. He wasn't laughing. Neither was Todd.

"We reckon that's a pretty good one, actually. It's going in."

"What's this 'we' all of a sudden?" Cassie flushed, annoyed at having her judgement challenged. "I'll decide what goes in and what doesn't and, as far as I'm concerned, stuff like that is just too fantastic. It's a horror story rip-off and makes the whole thing ridiculous…"

"That's what you think. Fraser reckons it's just what the punters want. They'll eat it up. Now, why don't you go away, Cassie, and leave us alone?"

"All right, all right. I was just offering my advice. And in my opinion…"

"We don't need it," Warren cut in. "Fraser and me are doing just fine without you butting in. We'll show you what we've got, when we've got it. You just get on with being editor."

"Right." Cassie went back to her own desk, miffed. "Where is he anyway?"

"Dunno." Warren shook his head. "He went to check on this Billy kid."

"What Billy kid?"

"Some kid," Warren explained patiently, "called Billy." He pointed at a leaning pile of papers. "All these ones start something like: 'Billy said' or 'Billy told me' and some of the stories are wicked, really weird. Fraser thinks the kid could be interesting, he wants to talk to him, so he's gone looking for him. Is that all right with you?"

"Fine. As long as everyone's busy." *Everybody except me*. Suddenly Cassie felt excluded from her own paper. She stood up. "Excuse me, I've got some photocopying to do."

The photocopier was at the end of the same corridor where Louise had undergone her terrifying "near death" experience, but nothing seemed strange this afternoon. There were no ghostly figures, no sudden drops in temperature, no weird white mists, no unexplained phenomena whatsoever as Cassie walked along the wood-panelled hall. The copier was on a landing looking down into the reception area, the part of the old house which had been the library.

It was not until Cassie had fed her card into the machine that she noticed the little red symbol was flashing. The copier was out of paper. She checked the tray. Empty. She checked the storage drawer under the machine: that was empty, too. She bit her lip, craning over the banister, trying to spot Mrs Weatherall or one of her assistants, but there was no one down there. The place was deserted.

Cassie looked towards the stationery cupboard and then went over and tried the door. To her surprise, it was not locked. She turned the handle, looking round quickly before going in. She was not supposed to be doing this. Pupils were not allowed to go into the stationery cupboard on their own in case they nicked stuff. Mrs Weatherall would blow a fuse at the very idea, but she wasn't there, was she? And it was not as if Cassie was going to steal anything. She was just going to get more A4 to fill the machine which would be of general benefit.

Cassie snapped on the light. Metal shelves lined the narrow windowless room from floor to ceiling holding a cornucopia of different coloured paper and card, packs of brand new exercise books. Cassie looked round, locating the A4. It was right at the other end, up against the far wall. She started down towards it, thinking that it was a daft place to put it, when the door swung shut. Cassie stopped. Behind her, levers slid and the bolt clicked quietly into place inside the mortise lock.

6

The lights went out just as Cassie got halfway down the long narrow room. The darkness was complete; an absolute blackness. Cassie blinked – once, twice – unable to tell if her eyes were open or shut. She had a sudden feeling that she was about to fall and put her arms out to steady herself, expecting to grasp on to metal shelving, but there was nothing there. The shelves, and the stationery they held, were gone. She turned round and back, telling herself not to panic, but she no longer knew which way she was facing, which way to go to find the door.

Cassie suffered from mild claustrophobia. She avoided lifts whenever possible, and small confined spaces made her feel funny, but she had never been trapped like this. The darkness became something you could feel and touch, scarfing her face, blocking her nose, blinding her eyes, filling her mouth like black angora. She could not breathe; it spread down into her lungs like invisible filaments, choking her.

She lost all sense of dimension; she was unable to gauge the space she was in at all. It seemed to distort and contract around her: one moment the walls were moving in, preparing to squeeze the life out of her, the next there was no space, no dimensions, just this suffocating darkness going on to infinity.

Cassie stood bathed in sweat, struggling for breath, fighting down powerful waves of nausea. Time seemed to stretch. She lost track of how long she had been in there. She thought she was going to pass out. She sank to her knees and began to crawl in the direction she thought was the door. The floor was wooden; splinters were digging their way into her flesh. The wall, when she found it, was bare brick; it bruised her forehead and grazed her knuckles.

She had no idea how long, or how far, she crawled until she found the door. Her fingers recognized the shiny mahogany and began rapping on it, then thumping, and a voice, at first small and croaky, grew stronger until it was screaming:

"Let me out! Let me out of here!"

Suddenly the door opened and she tumbled forward, blinded by the light, landing in a heap on a level with Mrs Weatherall's shiny brown court shoes.

"Why, Cassie," the school secretary reached down to help her up, "whatever is the matter?"

Cassie stood in front of her, pulling at her rumpled clothes. Her face was wet – she must have been crying. She sniffed and wiped her cheeks with her sleeve.

"I – I went to get paper, for – for the photocopier," she stammered. "I – I got locked in, the light went out. I don't know, I panicked…"

Mrs Weatherall looked at Cassie in astonishment. The girl standing behind echoed her amazement.

"But Cassie – the door wasn't locked, was it, Kirsty?" The girl shook her head as Mrs Weatherall manipulated the handle. "See? I have the keys." She showed Cassie the bunch in her hand. "And look," she switched the light on and off, "perfect working order."

Cassie turned back. The room was just as it had been when she went in. Brightly lit by neon strip, the shelves of stationery were back again and the wall behind was smooth cream-painted plaster. The floor was covered in grey lino tiles. She examined her hands for grazes and splinters. The knuckles were red from rapping on the door but otherwise there was not a mark on them.

"Pupils are not allowed in there, you know," the secretary added, leaning forward to lock the door. "Perhaps you better leave replenishing the photocopier to the staff in future."

With that she went downstairs, but Kirsty stayed behind.

"Are you sure you're all right?" she asked.

Cassie nodded.

"It's just that there's something I think you ought to know. She didn't believe it," she nodded towards Mrs Weatherall's retreating back, "but some of the girls, you know, the other secretaries and that, and some of us who help out, have heard kind of noises."

"What?" Cassie asked, trying to get hold of herself. "What kind of noises?"

"Funny noises. Coming from that room you was in. Like a kid crying. I even unlocked it once," the girl laughed nervously, "to see if someone had got stuck inside.

There was no one there, but none of us will go in now, not on our own. Just thought you might like to know."

"Yeah, thanks," Cassie said. Somehow, knowing she was not alone in experiencing fear in that room stopped her feeling quite so foolish.

"There's another thing." Kirsty reached down and pulled a wad of paper from the re-cycling bin. "See these?" The sheets she held were all black. "The photocopier was doing this just before you got trapped in there. Mrs W says it's the toner playing up. But I don't know. Look. Look closely."

Cassie took the copies one by one and held them towards the window. The blackness was not uniform. In the middle of each one was a five-pointed shape edged in white. It looked like a starfish. Cassie turned the paper round; either that, or a child's hand print.

"Can I have these?"

"Sure, help yourself. Take 'em all, but," she bit her lip, "if you put them in the paper – you know, in the Psi Files? – don't say I told you."

"Don't worry, Kirsty." Cassie managed the ghost of a smile. "I never reveal my sources."

Cassie leaned against the Coke machine in the corridor which led into the main teaching block. The bell had gone for afternoon school; the crowds of kids had thinned to twos and threes. She was dying of thirst but still shaking so much she could hardly get her money into the slot. The pound coin slipped out of her hand and bounced across the floor. Cassie closed her eyes in near despair when a voice by her ear said, "Here, let me do it for you. What do you want? Diet Coke do?"

She nodded as Jake fed the money in and punched the button. The drink thunked down. Cassie reached for it, rolling the ice-cold metal across her forehead. Her head felt as if it was about to split apart. Heat from the day was cooking the glass-walled corridor. It was like standing in an oven.

"Are you OK?" Jake asked, as she ripped the ring pull and gulped the contents.

"No." She shook her head, brown bubbles foaming across her white teeth. "Not really."

Jake shoved his hands deeper into his pockets and looked down at his trainers. She was going to feel even less OK when she heard this, but he had to say something. He admired her almost more than anyone else he knew and couldn't stand to see her made to look a fool. No one else was about to do it. He had to be the one to tell her.

"There's something you ought to know…"

"What?" Cassie took another swig. "Out with it."

"Not here." He took her arm. "Let's go for a walk, shall we?"

It was cooler outside. Cassie followed Jake through the deserted playground towards the woods. The school was set in magnificent grounds, and although the flowerbeds near to the school had been tarmaced over for play areas and car parks or beaten to concrete by generations of pounding feet, it was not far before you reached big trees and tall shrubbery.

The path led to a rickety bridge which crossed a small ornamental lake. Down here there were still reminders that this used to be a family home. An old gnarled willow tree shaded a little pet cemetery with a group of small stones dedicated to "Rover", "Duke", "Tibby". They were all properly carved and dated; the most recent was March, 1908. They must have been placed to commemorate pets belonging to the Campbell Roberts' children, but weeds had grown up, covering the carving and turning the stones into humps in the grass.

The lake must have been pretty back then, but now empty crisp bags and drink cans bobbed and floated on the scummy green surface. Over the bridge was strictly out of bounds. The carpet of litter thinned as the path wound on, passing from formal laid out grounds into genuine woodland. The sounds and sights of school life receded quickly. Squirrels chased up trees and pigeons called to each other through the green depths. Even though the nearest building was only a hundred yards away, it felt as though you were suddenly deep in the country. The woods went on from here, leading down to the river. The whole area belonged to the school; it had been willed to the council by the last of the Campbell Roberts family and was to be used by the children of the city in perpetuity.

Cassie walked on mechanically. What Jake was saying rendered her temporarily numb, oblivious to the lovely summer day and the beauty of their surroundings.

"Are you sure?" she said, after he fell silent.

"Absolutely." They had stopped in a clearing. Jake pulled a frond from a clump of undergrowth growing round a fallen tree stump and began stripping the leaves. "I don't know how he managed those stunts last week – you know, with Louise and the science lab and that – but all this poltergeist business… It's a scam, Cassie. Fraser fixed the bells and the computers somehow, and he got

Todd and Warren to turf that classroom and turn over the lockers."

Cassie nodded slowly. It figured. She remembered Fraser's effortless manipulation of the desktop publishing package, and his dad was "in computers". As for Todd and Warren, they would definitely be up for it. Their initial hostility towards the new boy had turned into something close to hero worship.

"You know what this means, if it gets out," Cassie said.

Jake nodded unhappily. With Warren and Todd involved it was bound to get out. The pair of them had mouths like the Euro Tunnel.

Cassie shut her eyes, pinching the bridge of her nose, anxiety arrowing lines down her forehead. She could see it all, flashing through her mind like a speeded-up video. Her credibility would melt like snow; she would be a total joke, not just now, but after she left, for years probably. And then there was the Head. The thought of him finding out made her feel sick. If he got wind of this, the merest hint, she'd probably be expelled; even if she wasn't, she could hardly expect a glowing reference. All her hopes for university, all that work, trashed.

It was not just the Head, what about all the others they had fooled? Like Louise – she'd be furious. It was not just Louise… Fraser and Co had played a trick on her, too. Cassie remembered the stationery cupboard, the photocopier. *I bet they had a right old laugh about that.*

"There's something else…"

"What? You might as well tell me. It can't be worse than that."

It was. Much worse. Cassie's fair skin flushed as Jake told

her, the high cheekbones washing red with humiliation. This was about her and Fraser. It was personal.

"I heard," Jake pushed his glasses up his nose, "I heard him talking to Todd and Warren about, about that time he took you out."

"What?" Cassie looked up sharply. "Nothing happened…"

"I don't mean like that." Jake shook his head. "It was a bet…"

"A bet! What kind of bet?"

"They said, they said he couldn't, um, pull you." Jake blushed to use their words. He didn't like associating Cassie with that kind of term. "And, and Fraser said he could – that's all."

"Oh, right. I see…" Cassie suddenly felt weak. "Oh, that's great! That's wonderful!"

"Maybe I shouldn't have told you," Jake said, after a while. "I didn't want to upset you…"

"No, you did right." Cassie sniffed and looked up at him. The tears sparkling in her deep blue eyes and the shake in her voice were there because of anger.

"We need to jack all this poltergeist stuff," Jake said, thinking it was best to change the subject, to take her mind off Fraser and the tricks he had been playing. "And all that Psi Files crap. Get back to real stories. Like that kid that went missing."

"Which kid?"

"Exactly." Jake frowned. "That's the point I'm making. Her name is Wendy Richardson. She went missing over a week ago, not far from here." He looked round, indicating the direction of the river. "Down by the weir, in fact, and *Orbit* hasn't even mentioned it. I was thinking maybe we could do a feature, about 'Stranger Danger' – not too frightening, but advising readers to be wary. We could find out what the police are doing, how the search is going…"

"OK, OK – I get the picture." She held her hands up, palms out, warding off any more reproaches. "You're right. That's the kind of thing we should be going for. I've kind of let myself get sidetracked." She gave a bitter little grin. "It won't happen again. Thanks for telling me, Jake." She took his hand. "You're a good mate. We'd better go back now, get down to some real work."

She let go of him and went to the main path. Jake stayed behind for a second in that still place, saving the moment to think about later. He looked down at the back of his freckled hand where he could still feel the grip of her fingers. Laughter filtered through the whispering leaves of the trees and with it came the rhythm of children chanting.

Cassie was waiting for him on the edge of the clearing. They both stopped and listened.

"What's that?" Cassie turned her head, trying to locate the place where the sound was coming from.

"Kids playing in the woods."

"Shouldn't they be in classes? They sound too young to be out in the afternoon."

"Could be from the junior school. They have a longer lunchtime."

A line of children appeared, slipping in and out of the trees, on a path parallel but below their own. Brightly coloured summer clothes identified them as primary school pupils. Students at Campbell Roberts wore uniform. Jake craned forward, anxious in case Amy was with them. He had told her not to play in the woods. Apart from the obvious dangers he and Cassie had just been talking about, there were other perils here. It was easy to get lost and some of the old quarry workings and mine shafts were not properly fenced off.

"What are they doing?" Cassie asked.

"Playing 'Seven Steps'," Jake replied.

The children were threading nearer now, the words of their song becoming more distinct.

"Come and play, come and play,
We're off looking for the Steps today!
The woods are dark; the grass is green,
You can't hide 'cos you've been seen!
If you don't come now, don't come at all,
We are meeting by the waterfall...
One! Two! Three! Four! Five! Six! Seven!"

The last part of the chant was accompanied by hopscotch hopping from one foot, to both, to the other foot, and so on, until the numbers were counted and the nonsense rhyme could start again.

"Come and play..."

Cassie had almost forgotten, but the familiar words, repeated over and over, brought it all back to her. She had played this game. All the kids round here played it, until they grew too old, then it passed on to the next ones coming up. It never went out of fashion. It was stupid, really, or seemed so to her now. One of those strange things young kids did that made them incomprehensible to grown-ups. One of the things that marked their world off from that of any adult.

Somewhere in the woods, so the story went, there were seven steps. If you found them, and went down them, you would die before you touched the seventh. That was it. She had spent months combing these woods, searching with her mates, singing the song, just like these kids here.

"What were your steps like?" Jake asked.

Cassie turned, surprised. He seemed to be sharing her thoughts.

"Oh," she laughed, embarrassed to be caught in this pocket of childhood. "They were marble, kind of carved and ornate, but green with neglect, as though they'd been left from some fabulous old ruined garden."

Jake smiled. "Mine were wooden. At the top they were solid enough, but the ones towards the bottom were wet and slimy, all full of holes. If you jumped, you'd go straight through..."

Cassie didn't need to ask "Where to?" Everyone knew. If you reached the seventh step you'd never be seen again.

"Kid in my class," Jake went on, "saw them as stepping stones, you know, across a stream or a river."

Cassie nodded, she'd never thought of that. Somewhere in their heads, everyone had their own vision of the steps. These were as many and varied as the children who played the game, and everyone who played shared the excitement of the search and the vague dread of actually finding the steps. There were heated discussions about what people would do. The bravest, or perhaps the most foolish, would walk down, stepping on all of them, one at a time, intent on proving the rhyme was a lie. Others would jump the last, seeking to cheat the fate that was promised. Whatever they said, most people would run for their lives if they found anything even vaguely like steps. When she was ten, wild horses would not have dragged Cassie anywhere near them. That did not stop her looking, though. She continued, off and on, until she was about twelve and began to realize that the only place the steps existed was in their collective imagination.

The procession strung out below them, maybe five or six kids. *They shouldn't be out here*, Cassie thought, *not on their own, and especially not now. Hadn't they been told about what had happened to that little girl?* But Cassie and her friends had been told not to play in the woods, and had taken about as much notice. It always happened to someone else, never to you. Jake was right. Time for a feature on "Stranger Danger".

Cassie leaned over, relieved to see that the group was turning back towards school. At the head of the line, like the Pied Piper, was a figure she vaguely recognized. He was leading them in a weird version of "Simon Says"; everyone behind was mirroring him, waving their arms when he did. They were skipping, hopping, jumping, weaving on and off the path, all their movements synchronized to his, all the while keeping up the chant until it began to sound faintly hypnotic.

"Who's that boy?" Cassie asked, frowning. "The one in front. I've seen him before…"

"He's always around. They call him Billy."

"The one Fraser was looking for?"

Jake shrugged, "Yes, I guess. What did Fraser want with him?"

"Something to do with his Psi Files. I wonder if he found him?"

Jake shrugged again. "That would depend on Billy."

"Come on." Cassie turned away from the dancing children and her remembered past. Thinking about Fraser brought back more immediate concerns. "We better go and see if we can do some damage limitation."

7

Cassie returned to the *Orbit* office to find only Warren there, no sign of Todd or Fraser. She didn't say a thing; she just sat down at the editor's desk and switched on her screen. Across the room from her, Warren watched in disbelief as the story he was finishing off for Todd began to unravel. The characters he had just typed were disappearing like so many rows of knitting.

"Oh, blimey! Oh, no!" he muttered to himself, meaty fingers pounding the mouse in a vain attempt to halt the damage. "If I lose this, Todd'll go ape!"

The expression on his big sweating face changed from puzzled panic to serious alarm. Cassie would have laughed, if she hadn't been so mad.

"Hey! What are you doing?"

He had finally figured out that her editor screen was the source of the destruction.

"How do you know it's me?" she said softly, smiling at the blank screen in front of her. "Maybe it's some kind of paranormal phenomenon." She stared across at him now, blue eyes sharp, her voice hard. "Like poltergeists, for example."

Warren knew from her look that the game was up. He slumped in his chair, idly clicking the mouse. "Me and Todd have spent all day writing that," he said, sulkily. "It was a good story."

"It was not. It was a crock, Warren. And you know it. The whole thing is a scam, from start to finish, isn't it? Isn't it!"

Warren pushed himself back from his desk, his features settling into heavy lines of sullen resentment. Finally he nodded. "It wasn't my idea…"

Cassie did not think for a moment that it was – Warren wasn't given to having ideas, not on his own – but she waited for him to go on. She wanted confirmation; she wanted to know, and Warren would tell her. He wasn't big on loyalty, either.

"Who's idea was it, then?" she asked, keeping her voice low and even.

"Fraser's." Warren folded his arms, the check material of his shirt strained across his wide shoulders. "But it was just a laugh, Cass. A bit of fun. No big deal…"

"Is that right?" Cassie swung her chair round to face him. "I've always thought you were pretty stupid, Warren, but it's only now I'm realizing just *how* stupid. You do understand, that if this gets out, we are all going to be a total joke. And then, when the Head finds out, and I'm talking *when*, not *if*, here, we *all* run the risk of being expelled. You, me, Todd, the lot of us."

"What about Fraser? It was his idea…"

"What does he care?" Cassie's eyes were blazing anger

now. "He's only just got here! He could leave tomorrow and it would make no difference to any one, least of all him! But what are you going to do if you get chucked out? You are halfway through your A-levels, with university applications coming up. Do you really want a letter from the Head dropping on the doormat, saying you're sacked? How d'you fancy facing your old man, telling him you've screwed up your chances?"

Warren didn't reply, he just sat looking even more miserable. His dad was big, like him, but had run to fat. He was proud of his son, particularly his sporting prowess. Warren was already captain of the football team and next term was tipped to head the First 15. He might even get a county place. Warren wanted to study sports science at university and his dad was all for that. He wanted Warren to go on, make the best of himself, take advantage of opportunities he'd never had. He would not be best pleased if all that went down the tubes, and he was prone to violent rages.

"I see what you mean," Warren said finally.

"Good." Cassie's tone was frosted with sarcasm. "Well, that's a start. Now, Wurzel…" She called him by his old junior-school nickname just to watch him bridle. He grimaced. He hated being called that, but he did not interrupt. "Unless you want me to go to the Head myself, you are going to tell me everything you know – right now."

Cassie sat, fingers steepled, as Warren ran through Fraser's plan from start to finish. It was brilliant in a warped kind of way. You had to admit, he had a flair for something. It would have worked, too, if he had not enlisted the help of Todd and Warren.

"Tell, me, Wozza…" Warren bowed his head. He liked this little better than the other nickname. "One or two points I don't understand. How did he manage the fire in the science lab?"

"Easy. Lifted the keys from a lab tech's coat. Taped a magnifying glass to the window, waited for the sun to come round and do the business."

Ingenious. Cassie had to give him that.

"OK. How about Louise and the ghostly mist?"

"First he nicked her inhaler, when she was in here talking to you, then he nipped downstairs and waited. When he heard her coming, he released this dry ice he got from the science lab when he nicked the keys. She saw it, freaked, and he came galloping to the rescue."

"What about the figures she saw, or thought she saw?"

Warren's broad forehead wrinkled in a frown. "I don't reckon he did that. They were her own contribution. She was so scared, she'd have seen little green men, Fraser said."

"And what about these?" Cassie brandished the black photocopies in front of him. "What about the little trick he played on me? Locking me in the stationery cupboard." Her voice was shaking now. "I bet you had a real good laugh abut that one, didn't you?"

"When did that happen?"

"At lunchtime."

"Todd and me was in here the whole time, working on that story you just wiped. It wasn't us, and I don't know anything about it."

Warren hid a smile. Locking Cassie in the stationery cupboard, what a brilliant trick! He smothered a laugh; he was in danger of cracking up. You had to hand it to

51

Fraser, he really was cheeky. He stared at the photocopies, trying to keep a straight face, looking at the curious white-rimmed hand in the centre of the paper.

"I don't know anything about this, Cass," he said, deadpan now. "I absolutely swear to it!"

Cassie didn't wait to find out whether Fraser knew about it or not. As he came in, she went out, passing by him like a freezing cold front. He didn't have to ask what had happened. Outside the afternoon temperature was nudging the nineties, but in here frost coated the walls; the atmosphere was well below zero.

"She's well pissed off with you, mate," Warren observed. "As from now all the poltergeist stuff is junked."

"How did she find out?"

"Search me," Warren held his hands out to display his innocence, "but me and Todd'll be wanting our tenners back."

"Does she know about the bet, too?" Fraser asked, concerned. That was more serious than the other news.

"I ain't sure. She didn't say..." Warren looked towards Jake who had just come in and was standing at the notice board, sticking little flags on to a map of the area, trying to look as though he wasn't listening. "There's one way to find out."

Warren was over there in two strides. He picked Jake up by the scruff of his neck.

"You told her, didn't you? You stirring little git. Did you tell her about the bet, too?" He shook Jake hard, jamming his head against the wall. "Give, or I'll..."

"What if I did?" Jake shouted back. "You had no right

to talk about her like that. And mind my glasses, you muscle-moron."

"What did you call me?" Warren spun Jake round and hoisted him a foot off the ground.

"You heard."

"Say it again and I'll bust your bins and ram the bits down your throat."

"Let go of him," Fraser rapped from the other side of the room.

"Why should I? Cheeky little sod deserves a lesson."

"Warren, I said let go."

Fraser didn't raise his voice, but Warren released his grip. He let Jake slide down the wall and turned to Fraser.

"I still want my tenner back."

"Not a chance." Fraser's grin was thin and tight. "So what if she found out? It was a fair bet and I won it." He swung in his chair. "What else did she say? What about the Psi Files?"

"Says you can do what you like with it. She even made a few painful suggestions. She's splitting the paper in half. We do our bit, she'll do hers. With the help of little Jakey."

Warren reached down and pinched the other boy's cheek.

"Lay off, Warren," Jake snarled. "Or I'll…"

"You'll what? You little four-eyed git. Go running to Auntie Cass?"

"No, I'll…" Jake was shaking with rage.

"Leave him alone. What else did you tell her?" Fraser was addressing Jake now.

"Find out yourself. I'm off home." Jake went out, slamming the door behind him.

"Never mind." Fraser shrugged and smiled. If he was fazed by what had happened, he didn't show it. "We can have two papers. Louise'll make me editor."

"I don't think so," Warren replied. "Not when she knows about the stunt you pulled."

"How's she going to find out?"

"Cassie, of course. If we ain't good boys, she'll blow the whistle on all of us. Louise'll be the least of our worries."

"Cassie won't do that." Fraser surveyed the papers on his desk. "Anyway, splitting *Orbit* could be a good thing. See who files their copy first." He picked up a pile of stories and let them drift down. "There's plenty here for us to be getting on with and they'll have to start from scratch."

Fraser was sorry Cassie felt the way she did about what he had done and sorry that she had found out about the bet, but it couldn't be helped. Fraser was not one to cry over spilt milk.

The bet was a trivial side issue; he had gone out with her because he had wanted to. As far as *Orbit* was concerned, he had acted for the good of the paper, to get them out of the mess they were in. He could explain it all, if she would give him a chance, but she wouldn't listen, wouldn't even talk to him. She needed to understand: if it didn't happen, make it happen; if it hadn't happened, make out that it had. That was what journalism was about. Where would the tabloids be without that? Trouble with Cassie … she had principles. For Fraser, principles and journalism were incompatible.

He was sorry for other reasons. She was very attractive, but it was not just that. She was clever and sharp, and cool, able to take flak and give it back. He liked that in a girl. In fact, he liked her rather more than was comfortable.

Perhaps this bust up was for the best. On Sunday, sitting in her garden with the summer heat diffused by dappled leaves, mellowed by beer, and with her so near, he had been this much away from telling her. About him, about Duncan, about all of it. So maybe this was a good thing. It didn't do to allow anyone that close in.

He turned the pages of the stories in front of him, focusing his mind back on to the tales of the strange, the mysterious, the unexplained. Maybe Cassie had a point. Perhaps some of them were a bit over the top. But, on the other hand, vampire children with steel teeth and claws for hands were a lot less scary than what could happen in real life.

8

Fraser sat back in his chair, raised his arms above his head to ease the ache in his shoulders. He had read through every single submission. The trash bin by his foot was full, but even accounting for that there was some good material here, very good indeed. There were three different files on his desk; scrawled across them, in spiky italic capitals, were the titles: SCHOOL, TOWN, and BILLY.

He flipped open the file marked SCHOOL. This was a haunted place all right. There were lots of stories: about the woods, the House, the grounds. Most were from kids, but not all. The caretaker, the cleaners, office workers, had all seen things. One was from a teacher. That was good. A variety of stories from different sources would strengthen the feature he intended writing. The teacher's story went like this:

It was after a Parents' Evening, and I was late, the last

in the hall. As I went out, I saw someone go through the glass doors into the House. He did not look like a member of staff, so I thought I ought to follow, in case it was a parent trying to find his way out. At that time of night I knew the front door would be locked. I went into reception, but found no one there. Thinking I must be mistaken, I turned to go, but then something made me look towards the stairs. There was a man walking up; he was treading slowly, holding on to the banister. I called out to him, but it was as though he did not hear; he just carried on climbing. It struck me then that there was something a bit odd about him. He was dressed in old-fashioned plus-fours and was quite elderly. He didn't really look like one of our parents. Just as he got to the top of the stairs, he turned round. He looked just like the Campbell Roberts portrait that hangs in the foyer! White whiskers, dour expression, everything. I couldn't believe my eyes! I glanced away, to check the painting, and when I looked back, the old gentleman had disappeared.

It would need jazzing up a bit, get rid of the teacher-speak, but it went nicely with the other cluster of stories Fraser had found related to the House. Two of these were remarkably similar to what had happened to Louise. They might be copycats, and he had been just about to dismiss them as that, but there were one or two crucial differences. Not least, the fact that these had not been stage-managed by him; these encounters had actually happened.

I read what you said about Louise in Orbit *last week and*

*thought you might be interested in this. Me and my mate
Sonia were up on top corridor when we saw this strange
mist coming towards us. It was so thick Sonia reckoned
there might be a fire but the alarm hadn't gone off or
anything like that. We were just going to go and tell
someone when we heard laughing, like a kind of
chuckling, and through the mist we saw a boy and girl
coming towards us. We thought they were kids from the
school and called out to them but when they got nearer we
could see that she was little, maybe six or seven. Not much
older than that. He was older, maybe twelve or thirteen,
but they was dressed in olden-day clothes. The mist
seemed to spread and thin out across the ground and as
that happened they seemed to thin out also. Me and Sonia
was really scared so we legged it down the stairs. Sonia
said not to tell anyone, so I didn't. But now I reckon it's
OK to say because that girl Louise has and she's in the
sixth-form.*

The letter was signed: *Andrea W. 10BN.*

Fraser put it on one side. He might try and track her
down for an interview. Anything that gave the Louise
story credibility might turn out to be handy.

The CITY file contained a wealth of stories from
people of all ages. Kids had written about things told to
them by parents, grandparents, neighbours, friends of
the family. Most only recorded the bare facts of the case.
To be of any use, they would have to be re-written. They
had the comfortable feel of tales often told; the chilling,
jolting detail, necessary to scare, had been worn away by
frequent telling, making the stories less than frightening,
more curious and absorbing. Still, he tapped his pen

against his teeth, the best possessed a kernel of first-hand experience that defied rational explanation, and that's what you had to have if you wanted to convince and intrigue the reader.

Fraser fanned the papers in the file. There was enough here for many issues of *Orbit*. The pattern of strange encounters, haunted places, unexpected apparitions, spread across the city like a giant web. Phantom coaches had been updated to ghostly lorries, but they still made occasional terrifying appearances, lights blazing, veering wildly out of control on the old trunk road running north to south. The headless horseman had become the headless motorcyclist, the lonely byway he used to frequent had become an industrial estate, but his figure was still glimpsed when the moon was full, riding the long perimeter road that ran round the edge of the brand new factories. The men who worked for the security firm, whose job it was to patrol the site, made sure their duties kept them indoors on those particular nights.

If the tales were to be believed, the centre of the city was thick with ghosts; they haunted shops, pubs, offices, making their presence felt even in cinemas and shopping malls. Everywhere you went, it seemed, the past underlay the present. Black monks and white nuns, ghostly processions in medieval robes, walked the old routes, threading their separate unseen way through the throngs of the living. Cartwheels crunched on cobble stones down streets long tarmaced. Horses's hooves rang in courtyards that no longer existed. Buildings at confluences of hidden streams endured generations of strange occurrences. Stories echoed up from mines long shut, the shafts filled up, the pithead covered by petrol stations and supermarkets. Miners, trapped below ground by some ancient accident, were still seen, Davey lamps swinging from their belts as they made their way to work, and their knockings and cries were still to be heard on dark midwinter mornings.

This was a rich archive, but to make sense of it, to really turn it into something, Fraser needed to know far more about the city: its geography, its history. He did not know the places mentioned; the street names and districts were unfamiliar. He went to the map pinned on the wall opposite. This was some help, but not much. It was covered with labels, for one thing, each made out in Jake's small, neat writing. The other problem was that many of his respondents assumed local knowledge, referring to the Butts, the Burgess, Bishopsgate, the Brideswell. They might as well have been writing about a foreign city. Some stories were specific to particular pubs or shops which weren't on the map anyway: Jordan's, West & Wise, the ABC, Nag's Head, Old Sun Rise.

Fraser turned away from the map and went back to his desk, flipping open the file with BILLY written across the top. The stories in here were extremely localized which made them even more difficult to decipher. They had been contributed by younger children and this made them hard to read. They described a mysterious hidden world of secret games and arcane activities which went on under the Old Bridge, by Stoke's, up the Fletch, in Black Spinney and Runghills Copse, along the ginnels down our end, and up the cut by Bishop's Clump. He wrote notes for a while and then stopped. He put his pen down and passed a hand over his eyes. It made no sense to him. It might as well be in Swahili. He was going to need help with this. Help from someone sharp and smart, intuitive and bright, someone with good local knowledge. The kind of help that was not going to come from two boneheaded jocks whose local knowledge extended to City's place in the football league. He needed Cassie.

He could do no more tonight. He swept up his notes, put the files under his arm, and headed for the door. It was later than he thought, there was no one on the landing or on the corridor, no sound from the reception area below. The staff must have all gone home. Somewhere in the main school a polisher rattled and droned, but the House was deserted.

Fraser stepped out from the foot of the stairs, boot heels ringing loud in the silence as he crossed to take the next flight down. Suddenly, in the middle of the floor, he stopped. He had a feeling of being watched, that there was someone standing behind him, but he had checked as he came down the narrow attic stairs and there had been no one in the corridor; the whole length of it had been empty. He turned slowly. The boy was standing an arm's length away. Fraser knew without being told that this was Billy.

"I heard you were looking for me," the boy said, without taking his eyes off Fraser's face. "I'm Billy."

"I know." Fraser stepped towards him, but the boy stepped back.

"What do you want?" he asked, eyes set deep in his small, pinched face. Shadows haloed the sockets with purple smudges. "What do you want with me?"

"Hey, don't be scared." Fraser put his hand out, but the

boy flinched, dodging away from him. "I just want your help, that's all. I'm not going to hurt you."

"Help with what?"

"These stories." Fraser flipped open the BILLY file. "Kids have written into the paper, into *Orbit*, and some of them mention you…"

Billy shook his head. His hair was dark and hung down in matted strands. It appeared to be filthy.

"You don't have to read them," Fraser smiled, thinking his reluctance might be related to his reading ability. "I just want to interview you, talk to you about them. We could do it now, if you like…"

Fraser took a dictaphone out of his pocket.

"Oh, no, no…" Billy held up his hands, to ward Fraser off, fingers extended in star shapes. The nails were bitten raw to the quick, the lines on the palms were etched and mapped with dirt, the spaces between the fingers crusted with grimy deltas. "I don't want anything like that!"

"OK." Fraser returned the machine to his pocket. "Take it easy! How about if you talk and I just write down what you say, how about that?"

"Yes. I guess that would be all right…" Billy nodded, smiling now, showing small brown-streaked teeth; two of the front ones were broken, others were blackened, eroded by decay. "Hang on…"

The boy cocked his head to the right and then left, as though following a sound only he could pick up, far beyond normal human range, quite outside Fraser's field of hearing.

He suddenly looked up.

"I've got to go now."

He made for the stairs. Billy was fast, but Fraser was

faster. He shot out a long arm as Billy went to dodge past and grabbed the younger boy by the shoulder. His fingers closed on the cheap cotton of his black bomber-jacket. The material was soapy to the touch, greasy with dirt. The sensation was so unpleasant Fraser nearly let go, but he hung on. For a moment he could feel the boy's shoulder, bird thin, then the cotton began to rip, disintegrating within his tightening fist. The T-shirt tore also, the fraying material splitting at the neck to show dirt-stippled skin and hollow collarbone.

Billy looked back, his eyes huge and black, the irises retreating to show all pupil. His face stretched tight, nose wrinkling, lips pulled back, as he winced at the damage.

"I'm sorry," Fraser said, hastily letting go. "I didn't mean to … I'm sorry…"

The boy did not say a word. He retreated across the corridor, holding his shoulder like a wound, trying to pin the torn fabric back from where it was flapping about like an open mouth. At the head of the stairs he stopped, and the last look he gave seemed heavy with reproach, freighted with accusation. Then he turned and was gone, leaving Fraser alone.

Fraser turned away, hitting the smooth cream surface of the wall with his fist. He punched paint to plaster until his knuckles were bleeding, but he did not notice. Depression swept over him, wrapping round him in thick black folds, fitting to his contours like a familiar coat he had just left off wearing. That kid was poor. Fraser had only seen poverty like that once before, when they were in Glasgow. The boy's clothes were dirty and thin because he lived in them; he had no changes. Now

Fraser had ripped his jacket, torn his T-shirt, when he clearly didn't have any others.

Fraser pounded his forehead gently against the wall. Why was it everything he did turned out wrong? Everything. He could not touch anything without it tearing, or breaking. Water squeezed from the corners of his closed eyes. Fraser realized, to his horror, that he was crying. Why cry for a stranger, when…? He leaned back, swiping the tears away with his sleeve. Why cry now, when he didn't cry then? It didn't make any sense to him. He looked down at his aching hand; his knuckles were bruised and torn but the pain was nothing to what he felt inside. Inside, he was dying. One little thing, and it came back again, just like the day it happened, perfect in every detail. All over a ripped bomber-jacket. Would he ever recover? The answer came back like a song's refrain, "Never, never". He would go on feeling this way for ever.

"Fraser?"

At the sound of Cassie's voice, he spun round as though he'd been shot.

"What's wrong?" she asked, from the top of the stairs. It was obvious something was, even from that distance.

"Nothing." He wiped his eyes again and cleared his throat, bundling his wounded hand down deep in his pocket. "What do you want?"

An apology would be nice, she was about to say, but the pain and unhappiness, so naked on his face, silenced her. The suffering she saw there made her feel as though she had intruded into a private place, as though she was the one who ought to be apologizing.

As she came towards him, she felt her anger, her fury at his behaviour towards her, receding. His deep anguish, his transparent despair, made her own feelings seem selfish and childish. She held out her hand.

"What's the matter? I can tell something is…"

"Nothing!" He thrust his own hands deeper in his pockets. "Honest." He sniffed and looked away. "It's that kid, Billy. He was here…"

"When?"

"Just now. You must have passed him on the stairs…"

Cassie frowned. She had not seen anybody.

"I ripped his jacket. I – I didn't mean to, it just happened…" Pain rippled across Fraser's face and he paused. "Like I told you, it's nothing." He swept his long dark hair back and managed a smile. "Are you still angry?"

"What do you think?"

"I'm sorry." He looked down at her, green eyes still magnified by collected tears. "I really am sorry for what I did. Sometimes," he shrugged, shoulders hunched, "I kind of get carried away, don't think things through. That bet – it's not how it looks. I wanted to see you, to go out with you, and they laughed, said I couldn't. That annoyed me. It was to do with them. It wasn't meant as an insult to you." He hesitated, trying to read her face, gauge her reaction. "Do you think we can wipe the slate? Start again?"

Cassie sighed. "Yes, I suppose so. But no more tricks – and positively no more bets…"

"Of course not. I promise." Relief flooded his face; his smile was radiant again. "From now on we play by your rules only."

"As long as that's understood."

"Absolutely." He took her arm. "I'm really glad you're

not mad any more, because I like you, Cassie. I really do. And I need your help."

"What with?"

"I'll explain on the way. Come on, I'll buy you a coffee."

Cassie allowed herself to be led out into the bright summer's day but a couple of things still troubled her. She had not seen anyone on her way up here. The front door was locked. No one had passed her in the corridor leading from the school; there had been no one in reception, or on the stairs. As for Fraser – she cast him a sideways glance – it wasn't just the stunts he'd pulled. There was something about him, something that had to do with his past, something he was keeping secret.

9

"The city has a long history…" Cassie looked out of the window of the small coffee-house. "There's been some kind of settlement here for more than a thousand years. In the Middle Ages it was particularly rich, with a castle, and the cathedral, and at least four great religious houses. That probably accounts for the number of monks and nuns people see. Most of the buildings are gone now, but they had cellars going on for miles and there are rumours of connecting tunnels. Everything here," she indicated the modern precinct, "has been built on top of something else. Every time they build anything there has to be a conservation dig. That new shopping mall for instance, the one we walked through? Work on that was halted for months while they excavated a medieval cemetery."

Fraser sat opposite, thinking over what she'd been telling him. He'd been right. She knew all about the area. On the way here she had shown him bits he'd never have seen in a million years; taking him down little backstreets, through cobbled courtyards, past a deep green depression which marked the moat of a castle no longer there. She had shown him ancient stonework, frilled with ferns, which had once been part of the town walls; pointed to a gap where a gibbet had once swung above a deep defile, right next door to a multi-storey car park.

The modern city went about its business, unconcerned with the older world which lay beneath its feet, skirting round and stepping over the few remains which still showed on the surface. A few lumps of masonry, broken pillars reduced to stumps, were all that was left now of the huge abbeys and monasteries which had once taken up most of what was now the city centre. Cassie showed him where the original stone from these great houses had been robbed and incorporated into later buildings. It made Fraser feel strange. If all that could disappear, what would be left from now? All these banks and shops, the precinct, and brand new shopping mall, the café they were sitting in: one day all it would add up to would be just another incomprehensible pile of rubble.

Even though it was hot, Fraser shivered as he gazed out of the window at the passing crowd. If anywhere was going to be haunted, this place was. In the maze of packed streets you could almost feel the dead jostling the living.

"What? Sorry, I was miles away…"

He turned his attention back to Cassie and what she was telling him. She was going through the notes he'd made from the Billy stories, identifying with ease the odd place names he had jotted down, the ones that had so puzzled him.

"The Old Bridge crosses the river just below the common. We used to call it the Troll Bridge, because it's a bit rickety-rackety and we reckoned there was something living under it." Cassie paused, gooseflesh creeping up her arms as she remembered the terror she'd felt crossing the rotting wooden slats, not daring to look down in case she met the cold unblinking eyes of the dark slimy thing whose home was underneath. "Stoke's Mill is a bit upstream. There's no mill any more, just a weir and a deep pool."

Stoke's Pool, above the vicious churning weir, had a surface like a dark mirror that seemed to want to suck you in. Many drowned bodies had been found in those still waters. Isolated and lonely, it was supposed to be a favourite spot for suicides. Anyone falling in up-stream was bound to fetch up there. If you stared long enough into those dark depths, so the story went, you'd see the faces of the dead, floating white and bloated next to your own. Cassie rubbed her arms as she looked down the list. Brideswell Pool had the same effect. That was right in the middle of the city, but its dull pewter surface seemed to take light in rather than reflect it, and people said it was bottomless. Stories clustered round all the places here. They all came back as Cassie read on. It was like looking at a route plan mapping out all the terrors of her own childhood.

"Black Spinney and Runghills Copse are part of the woods by the school," she told Fraser. "There's a pit in the middle of Runghills; kids go there to ride their bikes up and down the sides, but no one would go there at night."

"Why not?"

"They say it's a plague grave, a deep pit dug outside the city walls at the time of the Black Death to take the dead. So many died, they didn't have time to bury them properly. They just piled them all up and left them. Over the centuries the centre of the grave sank and the sides caved in, leaving the depression which is there now. It's all nonsense. The depression is probably due to quarrying, or collapsed mine works but," she shivered again, "it *is* a bit creepy. Dangerous, too. There are old mine shafts and tunnels all around that part of the woods. People shouldn't play there at all, but of course they do." She looked at the other queries on his list. "Ginnels are entries" – she grinned at his continuing incomprehension – "back alleys, the cut is the canal, and…" She looked at the last name. "Bishop's Clump is a stand-alone ring of trees at the top of the common. There are stories about that, too."

"Such as?"

"Well, nothing specific, but again, no one in their right mind would go there at night. It's rather eerie. There's a ring of tall trees, I think they're beeches, but you never hear any birds singing in them. The bypass isn't far away but as soon as you step into the ring, the silence is almost uncanny. It's like stepping into a different world. It's an ancient earthwork, and it is supposed to be on several ley-lines; maybe that accounts for it. There have been rumours of all kinds of things: witchcraft, unseen forces, even UFO sightings. All I know is one man stayed there all night and the next day they found him raving – well, that's what the kids say, anyway." She pushed the papers back towards him. "Will that do?"

"Admirably." Fraser put the paper back in his pocket.

"Thank you. One more thing, can you tell me where the seven steps are? Why are you laughing?"

"Nothing." Cassie shook her head. "You wouldn't get far without me, that's for sure. The seven steps isn't a place, as such, it's a game the kids play. Why do you want to know?"

"References to it appear in quite a few of the stories."

"May I see?"

Fraser handed her the relevant batch.

"Funny," Cassie said as she read through, "I was talking to Jake about it earlier today. Hey, this one's interesting. 'People say no one's ever found them,'" Cassie read out, "'but Billy says that's not true. A little girl he knew was playing in the woods one day when she came across the steps. She went down and down and no one ever saw her again. She vanished, like the earth just swallowed her, but she's not dead. She lives in another place with other little girls like her. That's what Billy says.'" Cassie frowned. "I never heard that before."

"What do you think of this one?" Fraser handed her another story.

"'I was down my gran's with my friend Sara…'" Cassie read. "'…we'd been playing 'Seven Steps' and Sara was singing the song. My gran went mad. Said we wasn't to play it, not ever, and not to go in the woods, neither. She said it wasn't safe. Over the years children had disappeared from them woods regular.' Umm…" Cassie frowned; the game went back much further than she had imagined. "Any more like that?"

"Yes," Fraser nodded, "a couple. Kids being told not to play it, warned about the woods, references to disappearances. They could just be bogeyman stories…"

"Even so." Cassie stared at the round writing, the conviction behind the childish hand. "It could be a promising line to follow up. Jake might like to do that."

"Does that mean you'll use them? I thought the Psi Files were dead in the water."

Cassie shook her head. "We asked for these contributions. We can't very well ignore them now our readers have taken the trouble to send them in. Anyway, they're interesting. What I meant was no more tricks, no more fabrications."

"I promise, scout's honour." Fraser held three fingers to his temple, green eyes sincere, expression serious. When he dropped the salute, he reached for her hand over the table. She did not move it away.

"I can see the funny side, though," Cassie said after a while. "Particularly Louise." She laughed and Fraser joined in. "It couldn't have happened to a nicer person. It must have been quite a giggle. And then there was me…" Cassie tried to keep up the jollity, but the memory of it still made her shaky. "That was a good one."

Fraser had begun to laugh along, but at her last words his grin died.

"What about you?"

"Me in the stationery cupboard."

"What stationery cupboard?"

"Earlier today. Lunchtime. You locked me in, remember?"

"I don't know anything about that, Cassie!" His hand tightened on hers. "I swear to you…"

"It must have been you. Todd and Warren are accounted for."

"It wasn't me, honestly. I was in with the Head of sixth-form nearly all lunchtime, going over my time-table. You can ask him if you don't believe me."

"What about these?"

Cassie held up the photocopies with the star-shaped hand, but she knew what his answer would be before she even showed him.

"I've never seen them before…"

They looked at each other, both thinking the same thing. When it started, the Psi Files had been a bit of a laugh, a way to boost sales, but now it was growing, taking on a life of its own. It was as though they had opened a door into some unknown, terrifying place and neither of them had any idea how to shut it, or any clue as to what might come through next.

10

Fraser paid and they left. Outside the coffee-shop, they almost fell over Jake, weaving his bike through the pedestrian area. They both said "Hello," but the younger boy just nodded and scooted away.

"What's up with him?" Cassie asked. It was not like Jake to be so unfriendly.

"He's probably pissed off with me." Fraser grinned. "Warren had a bit of a go at him on my behalf."

"Oh, no." Cassie grimaced; she knew what Warren could be like. "He didn't go over the top, did he?"

"A little. He does tend to get a bit physical."

Cassie stared after Jake, following his progress through the shoppers. "Maybe I should go after him…"

"I don't think so. He's a tough lad; he can take care of himself."

"But he might be upset…"

"Cassie! You're his editor, not his mother!"

Jake got to the end of the street and turned. He was

upset, but not by Warren, or even Fraser. He understood other boys, why they did things. No problem. He could deal with that. What he couldn't understand was Cassie. What was she doing with Fraser? Sitting in a café, holding hands with him, after what he had done to her? Girls. You think they're all right, and then they do something like that. He'd never understand them as long as he lived. Amy was OK, but she was only eight. Something happened to them around the age of twelve. She'd probably end up as daft as Cassie.

Jake watched them part on the corner and mounted his bike. At least she was not going home with him, that was one good thing. Cassie might be taken in by Fraser's charm and his handsome face, but what did they know about him? He'd just arrived from nowhere and suddenly all kinds of things were happening. Jake shook his head as he rode on. He might be the only one, but he did not trust Fraser.

Cassie asked Fraser over to her place, to continue working on the files. Jake might have been surprised to find that it was Fraser who declined the invitation. He was grateful for her help, and ordinarily would have jumped at the chance to spend more time with her, but he had business to do at home, and it had to be done alone.

The idea had come to him on his walk through the city. Part of him was listening to Cassie, taking in what she was saying, but another part was still clouded by depression, thinking about Billy, going over and over the confrontation with him, the way that pathetic jacket had ripped to show the grey fraying T-shirt, the dirty bare skin. Fraser felt bad about that, really terrible. The kid was bound to get into deep trouble when he got home. He wished there was some way he could make it up to him. Then suddenly, out of the blue, he knew what he would do. Once he had decided, he began to feel better, a whole lot better, like he had taken a painkiller and it was just beginning to kick in.

He left Cassie at the end of her road and hiked back to his place. He let himself in to the new detached house on the modern estate where he lived. It was just like all the others. A functional space with no personality, just a box to live in.

The house had been selected from a brochure, without any of them ever having seen it. It came part-furnished; that had been one of the attractions. The front window was shaded by Venetian blinds provided by the building company. The room behind was practically empty. A couple of chairs and a sofa stood on the beige carpet in front of a bare coffee-table and blank TV. The garden was already getting a straggly, parched, neglected look and they had been there less than a month. It stood out from the others, with their green, shaved lawns and manicured flowerbeds. Fraser wondered how long it would be before the neighbours began to complain.

Fraser let himself in, squeezing past the mahogany mock-Georgian front door and picking up the reef of mail and free newspapers that had collected behind it. He sorted through, dumping the junk and putting the rest on the hall table for Dad to see when he got home, *if* he got home. In the kitchen, the breakfast bar was covered in debris, spilt milk and cereal. Dirty dishes from the night before lay stacked on the counter waiting for someone to load them into the dishwasher.

He ignored them and went out again, mounting the stairs two at a time. The loft was reached by a trap door just outside the bathroom. Fraser reached up to release the light aluminium ladder. It came down with a rattling clang.

"Aleister? Is that you?"

His mother's voice, thick and slurred, came through the closed door of the master bedroom.

"Yeah, it's me," Fraser replied from halfway up the metal steps.

"What are you doing?"

"Just going into the loft."

"What for?"

"Got to get some books for school, for the courses I'm doing."

"Oh, right." Her voice came back faint and listless. Fraser could see her sinking back on to the pillows, eyes glazed and staring, any interest in what he was doing already erased by the drugs the doctor had prescribed for her. "I'm rather tired today," she went on, her voice fainter than ever. "I thought I'd have a lie-down. I left money on the table downstairs. I don't know what time your dad'll be back. Get some chips or something..."

"OK, Ma," Fraser shouted back.

You just stay where you are, he added to himself. If she knew what he was about to do, she'd really freak, but he was quite safe. There was about as much likelihood of her coming up here as climbing Everest.

The loft was stacked to the ceiling with trunks, suitcases and boxes still sealed up with tape with the moving firm's labels on them. They were all full of stuff that had never been unpacked. Throws and rugs and ornaments, photographs and pictures for the walls, souvenirs and nick-nacks. *Stuff from our life before*, Fraser thought bitterly, *stuff that would make this house into a home, like Cassie's, stuff from when we were a proper family*. That thought made him want to sink to the floor and just sit up there in the dust and insulating felt, but he pushed it out of his mind. He had something specific to do, something to look for. Concentrating on that could serve to hold back the fresh waves of depression which threatened to break over him.

He knew what he was looking for. A blue suitcase with the single letter D chalked on it. It was locked. Fraser used his pocket knife to spring the hasp and threw the top open. The things were there, just as he knew they would be. Clothes. All washed and pressed and carefully folded. They smelt fresh, of washing powder and fabric softener, but there was a faint tang of something else, a piney, musky smell, Fraser recognized as the body spray he used himself. He sat back on his heels, remembering how mad he got if he even suspected someone else had been nicking it. No good thinking that now. Fraser reached into the case and selected what he wanted.

The clothes were all labelled 9–10 years old. Billy must be older than that, but he was pretty undersized, so these would probably fit just right. Fraser removed a pair of Levis first: these had hardly been worn, the dark blue denim was soft and thick, velvety to the touch. Next he took out a couple of Gap T-shirts and a Stussy sweater. Then he chose a check shirt and a fleecy Berghaus alpine jacket. Delving beneath the surface clothes, he uncovered a layer of neatly folded underwear; a couple of pairs of pants would probably be a good idea. And trainers. He pulled out a pair of Nikes, caressing the leather, tracing the creases and folds with his fingers. These were a bit worn, and might be a size too big, but there was plenty of wear left, and their owner would not be needing them.

Fraser sighed and pinched the tears out of his eyes. That's twice in one day. He shook his head, trying to free himself of emotions that seemed to be droning about like bees, inside, outside. What was happening? He really had to pull himself together. He put the trainers at the bottom of the carrier bag he had brought up from the kitchen, then he folded the other items carefully and put them on top. After a moment's deliberation, he added a baseball cap and then he sat back. *These will do well, they will do very well*, he thought to himself. *Maybe tonight I can sleep properly, without having the dream again.* Fraser picked up the carrier and went down the steps. He would take the bag to school with him and deliver it in the morning.

Fraser did not sleep well. Perhaps it was the fish and chips he'd had, washed down with a big bottle of Coke, maybe it was the continued turmoil in his mind, but he woke up at just the same time, his bed clothes wrapped round him like soaked rags. He untangled himself and lay back on his bed, waiting for his heart to steady, the sweat drying on his body. He'd had the dream many times; it was always the same. Except tonight. Tonight there had been something different. He replayed it in front of closed eyes, going over the sequence of events in his mind, trying to isolate the difference.

He is high on a rock face, above the birds. Ravens and raptors circle on thermals well below him. The rock is close, streaks of quartz show white in its green-grey surface. He is clinging on, fingers and toes gripping, clamped into fissures and cracks. Above is blue sky, thin streams of white cloud running over the top of the crag. His father is in front, looking out the route, studying the complex interlocking planes in the rock for suitable hand- and foot-holds. Fraser is watching him climb, waiting to follow, when there is a cry from below. Fraser turns his head to look down. There's panic on the face looking up at him; his climbing companion has lost his footing. Instinctively, Fraser reaches out, nearly falling himself in offering his hand. He feels the other, smaller hand grasp on to his, but still the body is beginning to slip. *It'll be OK*, Fraser thinks because they are roped together, *the line will hold him*. He shouts up to his dad, and braces himself to be pulled off the face as, one by one, the small fingers slip out of his grip. Fraser watches, in slow motion. He watches the karibiner flip open; he sees the rope's bright weave: purple, white, mauve and green; he sees the knot capsize and slide, the knot Fraser himself had tied.

There is one shrill single cry, followed by his own voice shouting a name, as the figure below jerks free and begins to fall away, tumbling and turning, over and over, bouncing off crag and overhang, getting smaller and smaller, looking now like a dummy, now like a doll, until it lies on the ground, hundreds of feet down, sprawled like a broken Action Man. The name booms back in mocking echo, calling from mountain to mountain, calling to someone who will never hear it.

Then all sound fades. He remains on the rock face, frozen in time and space, with just the idiot whine of the wind whipping round him, tugging at his helmet, freezing the tears to his face.

That is the dream, and the dream is always the same, except this time, when it is different. Fraser plays it again and again in his head. It is the eyes that have changed, and the clothes. This time when he looks down, the face he sees belongs to Billy, and the body far, far below lies curled and limp like a little black crow.

11

Fraser stowed the plastic bag of clothes in his locker before morning school. He spent break and lunchtime searching for Billy, but no one seemed to have seen him.

Fraser sat through the first lesson of the afternoon in a haze of frustration, hardly listening to what was going on. He would need another approach if he was to find the boy. Giving him the stuff today had suddenly become important. He did not want to leave it all weekend in a locker that smelt of decomposing odour-eaters and old jock straps and taking it back home with him seemed like an even worse idea. That would be seriously bad karma. He leaned forward, head in hands, staring at the desk in an agony of impatience for the bell to go. An idea had begun to form in his mind, and he hated any kind of delay, anything that stood between him and a plan of action.

He was out of class before the bell had stopped ringing and caught up with Cassie just as she was on her way to another class.

"Cassie! Hey, Cassie! Can I talk to you for a minute?"

"Yes, sure."

Cassie peeled off from her group of friends, choosing to ignore the raised eyebrows and knowing grins as she left the mainstream and went with Fraser to the side of the busy corridor.

"I need your help."

Cassie looked up at him, folders hugged tightly to her chest. "What with? I thought we agreed to leave the stories until next week. I've really got no free time…"

"What stories?"

"For *Orbit*."

"Oh, no. It's not them. It's something else. I need to find Billy."

"What do you want him for?"

"There's something I – I want to check with him. I need to find him urgently. Please, Cassie."

Cassie looked at her watch.

"There's not much I can do now. I've got another lesson. Have you tried looking for him?"

"I've been all over. Asked everybody, even tried bribery. He's not around."

"Maybe he's not in school today. I'd say that was more than likely."

The school had a strict policy on truancy, but despite frequent crackdowns there was still a hard core of pupils whose attendance was sporadic, to say the least. Judging by his appearance, Billy could well be one of these.

"The best thing to do," Cassie added, "is find out what form he's in, and then check in the register."

"How do I get hold of that?"

"Go to Mrs Weatherall—"

"That's not going to work!" Fraser began to shake his head before the words were out of her mouth.

"Why not?"

"She doesn't like me. She thinks I'm a slacker." Fraser swept his long dark hair out of his eyes and smiled. "She likes you, though…"

"Oh, *I* see," Cassie nodded slowly. "How stupid of me. You want *me* to ask her. You had this all thought out, didn't you?"

"Well, sort of. I did ask a few kids, but none of them seemed to know what class he was in, so…" Fraser quirked an eyebrow, head cocked on one side.

"OK, OK," she found herself saying, "I'll see what I can do. It'll have to wait, though," she warned, "I can't do it until later on this afternoon."

"Whenever. Later's fine." Fraser seized her by the shoulders and kissed her. "Thanks, Cassie," he said, "you really are an angel, an absolute angel."

Then he kissed her again. *Just in case anyone missed it the first time*, Cassie thought, as she looked over his shoulder at the sea of passing faces turning in their direction.

Mrs Weatherall was out of the office but Kirsty, the girl Cassie had spoken to yesterday, agreed to help. Cassie stood behind the computer terminal as she brought up class list after class list. There were no Williams, Wills, Bills or Billys in the first three years of the school.

"How about second names?" Kirsty suggested.

So they checked them as well. Nothing.

"Maybe he's not at this school." Kirsty swung round on her chair. "He could be at the Juniors."

"Umm, yes." Somehow Cassie didn't think so, but it was worth a try.

"I'll give them a ring, shall I?"

"Yes, if you could," Cassie replied, looking at her watch. It was getting late, nearly time for the bell.

Kirsty listened for a moment and replaced the receiver. "It's on answerphone. They must have already gone home…"

"OK. Thanks, anyway." Cassie looked out of the window, just about to give up, when she saw Jake walk past with his sister. "Thanks again, Kirsty. See you."

She caught up with them by the gates.

"Jake! Wait!"

"What do you want?"

"There's something I want to ask Amy." Cassie leant down until her eyes were on the same level as those of the younger girl. "Tell me, Amy. Do you know a boy called Billy?"

Jake's sister nodded.

"Does he go to your school?"

"No, silly." Amy grinned, exposing a gap where her new teeth were growing. "He goes to *your* school, not ours. Everybody knows that."

"OK." Cassie stood up. "Thanks, Amy."

"What do you want to know for?" Jake asked.

"I don't. Fraser does."

Jake gave a little grunt of contempt. He might have guessed. Now Fraser had her doing his leg-work for him.

"Is that it?" Jake asked. "Because we're meeting Mum from work and then I'm going down the library."

"Which library?"

"The one in town."

"In that case, maybe you'd do me a favour." Cassie reached in her bag and took out a sheet of paper. "Can you check these out for me?"

"What are they?"

"Places mentioned in the readers' stories."

"What do you want me to find out?"

"I don't know…" Cassie shrugged. "Have a dig. See if you come up with anything interesting."

Jake looked at her, about to refuse. This was another one of Fraser's projects.

"*Please*, Jake…"

"Oh, OK." He stuck his hand out. "Give it here."

Jake took the list from her, barely glancing at it before stuffing it in his pocket.

"Thanks, Jake. See you."

"Yeah."

Amy waved but Jake did not look back as he went on down the school drive, steering his bike one-handed, the other arm round his sister, protecting her from the jostling mob. Cassie frowned as she watched them go. The way Jake was acting, verging on hostile, was almost certainly to do with Fraser. Cassie was quite aware that the younger boy had a crush on her, but she genuinely liked him and really didn't want to hurt him. She would have to talk to him, find a way to explain. About what? Fraser? Cassie shook her head. That would be difficult. She was pretty confused herself.

Cassie wondered about Fraser. Why was he still looking for Billy? Why did he need to see him so urgently? She had that feeling again: there was something odd about Fraser, something he was hiding.

Something mysterious.

Like Billy. Cassie looked at the children streaming past, some known to her, some not, but they were all in somebody's form. All except Billy. He was a familiar playground face, but his name was not on anybody's register, not on any list; he was not in the system at all. Probably no one had thought to check before. Cassie stared down the drive at the crowds making their way home, half-expecting to see a small, thin, black-clad figure weaving and dodging in and out of them. Billy exists. People see him around, maybe not every day, but often enough. So who the hell is he?

"You Fraser?"

Fraser turned at the tug on his sleeve and found a small boy looking at up at him from under a spiky, blond fringe.

"Yeah, that's me."

"You looking for a kid called Billy?"

"Yes, I am, as it happens."

"Well, I know where he is."

"Right now?"

"Yeah, right now."

"So? Tell me."

The small boy did not reply, simply held out his hand. "They said you was paying. For information."

"Well, that depends."

"On what?"

"The information. Tell me where he is, and I'll see."

"A quid."

Fraser shook his head. "50p."

"No chance," the boy laughed and withdrew his hand. "See you."

"No! Wait!" Fraser called him back. "All right, all right." He dug into his pocket. "Here you go. A quid it is," the coin spun up from his thumb, "now, where is he?"

"Down by the bike sheds," the boy snatched the coin from the air, "least he was a bit ago. No telling where he is now. See you around."

The boy took to his heels and was gone, melting into the crowd surging towards the bus stop.

Fraser held the carrier bag close to him, trying to figure out if it was a wind up. Maybe. Maybe not. Only one way to find out. He grabbed a little lad as a troupe of them came scurrying past.

"Hey, mate, I'm new round here. Can you tell me where the bike sheds are?"

"Over there," he gestured to the top of the school, "past the staff car park."

"Thanks."

Fraser dropped him back in with his friends and loped off in the direction indicated.

From the bike sheds, Fraser was directed to the bus stop, from the bus stop to the shops, from the shops to the multi-storey, from there to the car park at the back of Sainsbury's, and then on to some wasteground by the disused factories. At this point Fraser stopped, ready to call it off, deciding it really was a wind up after all. The carrier bag dangled from his wrist as he leaned on his thighs trying to catch his breath. The day was close; he was soaking, T-shirt plastered to his chest. He was being jerked around something chronic and it was too hot to be running around all over town. Time to give up and go home.

Then something made him look up. He caught a movement behind a clump of bushes way across the scrub-land. Even from this distance, Fraser knew it was Billy. The boy took off like a hare but Fraser was after him. Billy had a good start and ran fast but Fraser's legs were long, his stride wide, he was gaining all the time. He was nearly on him, when Billy scaled a crumbling concrete wall and disappeared out of sight.

Fraser stumbled, catching his foot on a tangle of rusting wire which lay hidden in the grass. A thick spike tore his trousers and ripped into his leg, but Fraser didn't even notice. He jumped for the top of the wall and pulled himself over, dropping down into the car park of a multi-storey block of flats. The space was deserted, apart from the remains of a couple of old cars. One had been burnt out, the other rested on its axles, stripped down to the chassis. No one would be driving those out in a hurry.

Fraser looked up at the flats rearing above him. A riot of graffiti scrawled across the base of the building. Most of the windows were boarded up, here and there the boards had been prised off and the glass smashed. Only the windows above stone-throwing distance remained intact. No one could live here, surely? Maybe Billy had dodged round the flats and gone on, but somehow Fraser didn't think so. He had a strong feeling that the boy had gone in here, had gone to ground.

As he stared up at the building he began to get an even stronger feeling, a feeling that someone was watching him. He looked towards the basement grille and, for a second, he thought he saw eyes gleaming in the darkness there: little beads of light, glinting ruby-bright, like an animal caught in headlights. But when he went nearer, the eyes disappeared and he could see nothing.

12

Fraser went round the building towards the front. The doors were boarded up, but on one side the wood had been pulled away. Fraser pulled it some more. Thick glass plate lay smashed on the floor; he stepped over that and into the foyer.

It was dark inside; it took time for his eyes to adjust to the light. Filth and debris littered the floor, lying in drifts up as far as the lift doors. These were open; Fraser went over and found a dark hole. The lift shaft gaped, the lift stuck permanently somewhere up round the fourth floor. Below him, blackness yawned. For a moment Fraser saw, or thought he saw, those little red sparks of light again, peering up at him, but when he blinked, they had gone.

Fraser backed away, groping for the stairs. His foot squelched down on something soft and unspeakable. Fraser gave a grimace of disgust and scraped his boot on the stair; he would be careful where he stepped from now on. It smelt bad in here, it stank of urine and rotting rubbish. *The boy can't live here,* Fraser told himself as he mounted the stairs, *no one could live in a place like this.*

He went down one long corridor after another. It was easy to get into the flats – all the doors had been smashed. He stepped over broken and splintered wood into the kind of devastation only normally seen in a war zone. Plaster hung in crazy chunks; it looked like someone had attacked every available surface with a sledgehammer. Everything of any conceivable use had been stripped out: pipes, sink units, electrical wiring. The toilets had been stopped up with cement, dust lay thick everywhere; no one had lived here in an age. The odd newspaper, old and yellowed, lay curled up in a corner, a mug with no handle sat on a windowsill, a child's broken plastic toy had been left, discarded, on a bare concrete floor, but there were no signs anywhere of recent occupation.

On the third landing, a steel grid barred the way to the remaining floors. The bars were thick and close together. Nothing above the size of a mouse could get through, certainly not a kid, even one as small and thin as Billy. Fraser turned back with relief. There was only one place left to go now; the only place he hadn't been, down in the basement.

Fraser went over to the entrance marked "Basement" and pushed the steel door, half-expecting it to be locked, but it wasn't. It swung easily, silently, as if the hinges had been oiled recently. The door opened inwards, flat against the wall, so Fraser could not see the marks on the dull grey paint, long scratches scored deep enough to reveal bright, silver metal.

He went to take the first step, then stopped. It smelt bad down here, real bad, far worse than the rest of the flats. Fraser's nostrils twitched and flared, picking up the sweetish rotten-fish stench of decaying flesh. It smelt like something had crawled in here to die. The smell made him want to gag.

Fraser leaned forward, peering into the darkness. It was as black as pitch. He wished he had a torch; without one it was impossible to see past the second step. How could Billy be down there? He would have to have the eyes of a cat.

Fraser shook his head and was just about to turn back, dismissing the whole escapade as stupid, when he heard something: a rustling, a kind of whispering. He thought he heard someone calling his name. There was definitely someone, or something, down there. He'd been wrong. The boy must have night vision. Who else could it be but Billy?

He was just about to set foot on the first step, when someone yanked him roughly backwards. The attack was sudden and the arms pulling at him were unexpectedly strong. Fraser staggered back into the foyer, fighting to keep his balance. The door in front of him slammed shut and Billy darted forward, bolting it at the bottom. Fraser just stood, so dumbstruck with surprise that he failed to notice that the bolt looked new and clumsily applied, or register how strange it was to secure a door like that from the outside. He did not think any of those things as he looked down at Billy.

"There." Billy stood up and looked at Fraser. "Now, you must leave this place. It's not safe. It's dangerous."

"I can see that," Fraser replied, looking round at the

litter and broken glass strewn across the floor of the foyer.

"That's not what I mean," Billy said, his small face screwed up with an impatience bordering on panic. "You can't stay, you mustn't."

"OK, OK." Fraser held up his hands in surrender. "I only came to find you. I have no intention of staying."

"Good. That's good." Billy managed a thin discoloured smile. "But you better go now." His head flicked round, again with that odd tilt, as though following a sound that no one else could hear, piped only into his ear. "Now! Go now!"

"I'm going, I'm going! Here," Fraser disengaged the carrier bag from his wrist, "I came to give you this. Catch. I'm sick of carting it around with me." He threw the plastic bundle to the boy and turned to go. "See? I'm out of here."

Billy looked at him, eyes all black-dilated pupil. He was still listening intently and now Fraser, too, could hear it. Maybe it was rats or cats, feral creatures who forage and make use of the waste and rubbish humans discard, but it sounded like the pattering of many light feet, and the *scritch, scritch, scritch* of what could have been claws on a metal surface. It was coming from the other side of the bolted door. Suddenly Fraser didn't need any further urging to leave.

Fraser limped off across the uneven wasteland. His leg was beginning to throb now and a quick inspection revealed an ugly four-inch gash up his left shin. He had noticed nothing when he was walking round the flats, but the bottom of his torn trouser leg was stiff with dried blood. His sock was soaked, too, and his boot squelching. The wound was still oozing a little bit. He carefully turned the cuff back down, trying to remember when he'd last had a tetanus jab.

"Fraser, Fraser! Wait up!"

Billy was shouting, running over the hummocky ground. Fraser stood and waited for him.

"I came to say thanks," the boy gasped, his thin chest heaving as he waved the bag. "It was kind of you. A kind thought."

"That's OK." Fraser shrugged and moved to go, suddenly embarrassed by his own generosity.

"Wait, wait!" Billy touched his arm. "There's something else. He says, he says to tell you it was an accident, it wasn't your fault. He says to tell you that you're not to go on feeling bad about it. He says to take care…"

"Who says? Who says that?"

Fraser's voice sounded far away, distant even to his own ears. His mouth felt numb, all his features seemed suddenly frozen, brittle, as though he'd been dipped in liquid nitrogen.

"Who?" he asked again, turning slowly towards Billy now, all movement taking an immense effort. "Who says it?"

"Duncan, of course," Billy replied. "Your brother."

The world lurched, tilting at the mention of his name. Fraser swallowed down nausea and put his hand out to clutch on to Billy, anything, to steady himself. He touched thin cloth, a bony shoulder, but his hand closed on air. In the blink of an eye the boy had gone.

Fraser stared round. Billy was nowhere to be seen.

Fraser looked down; it was as if the ground beneath his feet had swallowed the boy up. He turned round and round, suddenly feeling alone and small in the desolate landscape. Nothing stirred. The whole area, as far as the eye could see in every direction, was silent, deserted, from horizon to horizon. The boy had vanished.

How could that be? How could he just disappear like that? And how could Billy possibly know about Duncan? How could he even know that Fraser had a brother? Let alone that brother's name, let alone that his brother was... Fraser made himself say it: that his brother was dead. How could Billy know any of that? Who was he? *What* was he?

Above him, windows reflected sky, blind and malign. Fraser stared up, questions swarming in his mind, until it seemed as though the whole block was about to fall on top of him. Maybe Billy had gone back in there. Fraser limped over to look, but nothing seemed disturbed inside the broken doors, just his own boot-prints crossing the dusty filth-strewn floor. No sign that anyone else had been there at all.

There was no sign of him in the car park either, or in any of the garages. To the left of the flats was a little row of shops. Most of these were boarded up, but at the end, occupying the corner space, was a little café. The proprietor was standing in the open door, taking a breather, scratching his belly.

"Have you seen a kid come past here?" Fraser asked. "Dressed in black? About so big? Maybe eleven, twelve?"

The man just shook his head and turned away, leaving Fraser alone again in the empty street.

*   *   *

Fraser stumbled on in a daze, moving in a world where nothing seemed real, least of all himself. He could not recollect how long he had been walking around like this. He'd given up his search for Billy and begun to wander aimlessly, going on and on, round and round in circles. The light was fading before he woke to the fact that his leg hurt so much he could hardly walk and he was lost. He had no idea where he was. He did not know this part of the city.

Every phonebox he came to had been vandalized. Finally he found a phone in working order and punched in his number.

"There's no one here right now to take your call…"

What a surprise. He swore down the phone, yelling for his mother to pick up, but the message droned on to its conclusion. Fraser slammed down the receiver without waiting to leave a message. What was the point? She wouldn't listen to that, either. He stood for a moment, his throat closing in, the whole of his chest tightening. He fumbled in the pocket of his coat, took a blast from his inhaler and stood, head against the cool glass, waiting for his breathing to clear. Then he tried another number, one he had written on the back of his hand.

"Hi, is that Cassie? Oh, thank God. It's me, Fraser. Listen, I need your help again. I've had a bit of an accident…"

"Where are you?"

"That's the problem. I don't know exactly."

"See if there are any road signs, or any landmarks…"

Just hearing her voice saying sensible things like that

seemed to calm him down. Fraser looked outside and suddenly saw things he hadn't noticed before.

"The road sign is part bust off, but it looks like Longsomething," he said. "There's a pub on the corner, the Old Sun Rise, and I'm opposite some old red brick building that's all boarded up."

"OK, hold on."

Cassie went off to consult with her mother and between them they managed to locate him. He was in Longfield Road, at the back of the General, the old Victorian hospital which had served the city until all services had been transferred to the new Trust place on the outer ring-road.

"OK. We reckon we know where you are. Stay there and we'll come and pick you up."

Fraser went out and leaned against the phonebox. The day was still warm, but he found himself shivering. He used his inhaler again. Maybe it was wandering all over town and getting lost, or shock from cutting his leg, or maybe it was reaction to Billy and what the boy had told him, but his asthma had suddenly worsened. He hugged his coat to him, chest wheezing, as he looked up and down the street.

There was no one else on the long curving road in which he was standing; all around him was deserted, but again he had the strong sense of being watched. He found himself casting nervous glances over his shoulder. Time was dragging. He looked at his watch, unable to believe only a couple of minutes had passed since he was talking on the phone. He hoped Cassie would come soon; he was beginning to feel distinctly uncomfortable. His eyes kept being drawn back to the grim building opposite. The sun had begun to sink behind the steeply peaked roofs and shadows were creeping across the tarmac towards him.

The tall wrought-iron gates were shut. Weeds grew in the yard behind. The windows, set high in the soot-stained brickwork, were boarded and blind. There was obviously no one in there, how could there be? Fraser stood opposite, studying the building, when suddenly he had the same strange feeling that had come over him at the entrance to the basement in the multi-storey block of flats. It made no sense, he knew it was crazy, but he was tempted to go over there and have a look round.

A broken sign above the side door said: "Pathology". Stairs and lifts went down from there to a long corridor which led to the mortuary. At intervals ventilation grilles, and small panels of thick greeny-white glass, showed at street level. Some of these were missing: some might have been kicked in, some removed deliberately. From here, watchers could see out without being seen, and it was from here that the eyes were focusing. Not one pair, but many, sparking into life like little sets of red lights.

They observed him with avid interest. Pack-hunting animals, like hyenas and jackals, are vulnerable by themselves, but together they are far more dangerous than even the largest of predators. Like dogs, or wolves, these watchers acted together and were experienced in picking out the young, the weak, the vulnerable. Fraser was new to the area, unsettled, unhappy, the sort of boy who might run away, take off one day to become just another missing-person statistic. His arrival at the block of flats was no accident; he had been deliberately lured in there. Then, at the last minute, the watchers had been cheated. They did not intend for that to happen a second time.

Here he was again, wounded, alone. The attention focusing on him thickened and intensified until it became almost audible; a high-pitched psychic humming. Over the wasteland a dog whined, cringing back to his master's side, as Fraser began to cross the road.

13

Cassie and her mother drove up just as Fraser was stepping into the shadow of the old hospital. Cassie wound down her window and called to him, but he just went on walking. Cassie's mother pipped the horn and Cassie had to call out twice more before he turned round. He stared at them through the windscreen, as if waking from a dream. Cassie got out and opened the door to help him into the rear passenger seat. The atmosphere in the empty street seemed heavy, oppressive, charged with electricity.

Mrs Johnson felt it even in the car. "Feels like there's a storm coming," she said as her daughter got back in, and wound up her window even though there were no clouds to mar the deep blue sky.

She revved the little VW. Over the engine's full throated roar, none of them heard the strange humming, or noted the change in pitch and intensity as it turned into a keening scream – a howl of collective frustration.

*   *   *

"Hi. It's me." Cassie played with the cord of the phone, stretching it and letting it go, something she did when she was nervous. "How are you this morning?"

She had phoned him as soon as decently possible. She had been so concerned about him that she had nearly called in the middle of the night, just to check that he was all right. The only thing to stop her was the thought that his mum and dad might not appreciate having their sleep disturbed.

After they picked him up, Cassie's mum had taken one look at Fraser's injured leg and declared he would have to go to Casualty. They had sat with him for what seemed like hours, and all that time he didn't say a thing about what had happened to him. Cassie knew enough not to push him for explanations, but that did not prevent her from worrying about him and the state he was in. They dropped him off at his place, his wound cleaned and dressed; Fraser only spoke then to thank her mother. He had limped off up the drive, moving like sleepwalker.

"I'm fine." The answer came back down the phone-line. "Never felt better."

"Oh." Cassie felt deflated; she hadn't been expecting quite such an up-beat response. "Because I was worried…"

"Hey! Don't be! I'm OK now, honestly. But thank your mum for me, and thanks for coming to get me." He paused, and then said again, "Thanks, Cassie."

"It was no trouble," Cassie smiled. He could keep his secrets. She was just glad he was all right – and it was nice to be appreciated. "Does your leg hurt?"

"Nah. Not now. Aches a bit, that's all. Just needed a good night's sleep…"

"Did you get it?"

"Yes. I did, as it goes." He sounded surprised, as if it was not something that usually happened. "What are you doing today?" he added after a moment.

"Oh, Jake just phoned. He wants me to go down town with him. Follow up a story he's just heard on the local radio."

"What story?"

"About that little girl who's missing. Wendy" – Cassie stretched her mind for the name – "Wendy Richardson. Some people reckon they saw her last night, not far from where you were wandering about, in fact." She stopped and then went on. "Do you want to come? We were just going to ask around, see what's happening. You don't have to, though, if your leg is hurting or anything."

"It's not. I just told you." Fraser hopped off the stairs. "Give me quarter of an hour. I'll come round to your place."

A girl answering the description of Wendy Richardson had been seen the night before walking near a playground not far from the city centre. Police officers moved among the swings and roundabouts, questioning mothers sitting on benches, talking to the children who had come to play on the brightly painted seesaws and slides.

Dog-handlers fanned out across the surrounding wasteland, their charges sniffing and straining. It was a big area to search, stretching from the ring-road to the canal basin, a neglected pocket of the city fringed by old works, derelict factories, lock-ups and warehouses. It was ear-marked for development; hoardings announced the city's intended plans, presenting an idealized vista of low-rise housing, with shopping areas and an entertainment centre all set in an attractive landscape. However, that was still a dream in some planner's head. Bind weed grew up the legs of the billboards; the sun and rain had bleached the artist's impression to almost nothing.

There was no sign of Jake, so Cassie and Fraser joined a group of police officers standing on the edge of the wasteground. They didn't seem inclined to talk much, just to say the sighting was good. Some of them moved off to make enquiries in the surrounding multi-storey blocks of flats. Fraser and Cassie joined in with the ground search. They were looking for anything odd, anything out of place, an item of clothing, anything suspicious. They were searching for something else as well: something not mentioned, something left unspoken. They were looking for a body, and everyone out there was praying, hoping against hope, that they would not be the one to find it.

They found lots of things. Filthy mattresses, split and stained with the stuffing sticking out; old cookers; gutted washing machines; abandoned fridges. These were carefully opened, in case the child had crept in, in case a handy hiding place had turned into a coffin, but all of them were found to be empty. There were the ghastly remains of dead dogs and cats, nests of black bin-bags, tied tight, bulging shiny in the hot sun, or split and spilling their stinking contents. All these were carefully examined and found to contain nothing but rubbish. The search led on, away from the play area by the multi-storey blocks of flats back towards the centre of the city.

Cassie and Fraser crossed under the huge overarching struts of the ring-road and found Jake by the open expanse of water that was Brideswell Pool. The wide lake was so perfectly circular that it looked manmade, but it had been there time out of mind. Some said it marked the true heart of the city. Some said it was bottomless; whatever the truth in that, it had never been known to dry up. It had been the main source of water supply for many centuries and in World War Two it had provided water for the hard-pressed fire service.

Now it was a pleasant amenity. The gardens round it provided a cool stretch of green right in the centre of the city. At one corner stood Chapelgate, one of the remaining medieval city gates. A small sandstone church stood perched above massive stone walls, its dusty, pointed Gothic windows caged with wire to guard against inner-city vandalism. It had a gloomy neglected air about it. Recent attempts to make it into a workshop and art gallery seemed to have come to nothing. Its thick oak door was firmly shut.

The pool itself was the focus of police activity. The fishermen, who usually occupied pitches round the edges, had been told to pack up and go. Ducks, geese and swans stood discomforted on the dry cracked banks, pecking grumpily at thin patches of grass, as police frogmen in bulky suits swam slowly up and down, their broad flippers disturbing the surface of the dark muddy waters.

Cassie, Fraser and Jake stood watching the divers' progress as they criss-crossed the lake. Occasionally one would come up like a seal and shake his sleek rubber head, or give the thumbs-down to the men waiting in boats by the side. They had been here since early morning and had so far found nothing.

They were walking around to the other side, when suddenly Jake stopped. He squatted down, pushing his glasses up his nose, and peered at a large sluice gate.

"What are you doing?" Cassie and Fraser leaned over to see what he was looking at.

"That drain."

Jake pointed. A dried-up channel led to a round arched tunnel with a grey galvanized grid over the entrance.

"What about it?" Fraser asked, puzzled by the other boy's sudden interest.

"It's one of the ones I photographed."

"So?"

"Back then, I'm pretty sure the grille was tight shut…"

Fraser shrugged. "I still don't get it."

"Now it's open."

"Not by much."

"By enough." Jake stood up, dusting the knees of his jeans.

"Maybe workmen have been down there, taking advantage of a dry spell, cleaning it out, or something."

Jake frowned. "Maybe. But they would have to be pretty small ones. Midgets almost."

Fraser looked again. He was right, there was not enough space for an adult man to get into that space, or to enter the channel behind it.

"What do you think? That the kid went in there?"

"No," Jake shook his head, "not necessarily."

He could not explain what he thought, not in so many words, not exactly. It was just that since he'd taken the pictures of all the tunnels, he couldn't stop thinking about them. They were under his consciousness, surfacing in dreams, in idle waking moments. He had re-visited a few of them and each time he'd noticed the same thing. A change in the position of the grilles and grids. Some were open that had been closed, and vice versa. And some had to have been opened from the inside; there were places where no other explanation was possible. It seemed as though these were the openings to some hideous underground Wonderland; the entrance and exit holes of some demented White Rabbit.

He jumped on his bike and pedalled off. Cassie called after him, asking where he was going.

"The library," Jake shouted back.

"Oh, right. Don't forget the list."

"Which list?"

"The one I gave you last night."

"I'm doing it! So long."

Jake sped away before she could question him further. He had done nothing yet about the places Cassie had given him to check, mostly because the list did not originate with her. He had the paper with him, though. He would look into it as soon as he got to the library. He didn't like lying to Cassie.

Jake locked his bike to a stand outside the City Library and Records office and headed in through the double doors, making his way to the Local Reference section. He spread himself out over one of the big tables. He had more than enough space to work. This part of the library was more or less deserted; no one else seemed to want to spend a sunny Saturday shut up with a load of dusty old tomes.

Whatever his promise to Cassie, Jake did his own research first. By mid-afternoon the table was covered by mining surveys, underground maps and blue-print plans of the city. Jake sat hunched over a photocopied ordnance survey map, underlining names, highlighting the places which marked his tunnel entrances and exits. Cassie's list was on the table next to him. He flattened it out, examining it carefully. The places were written in spiky italic writing he took to be Fraser's and underneath Cassie had added in her neat sloping hand: "These are the sites mentioned in Psi File stories. Check them out for locality/potential pix/general spookiness!"

The Old Bridge
Stoke's Mill/Stoke's Pool/Weir
Black Spinney (disused colliery?)
Runghills Copse
Bishop's Clump
Seven Steps

The last one was scored through. Cassie must have crossed it out.

The second list consisted of places in the centre of town:

Odeon Cinema
Old Sun Rise
Fieldgate Lanes (Shopping Mall)
Lower Precinct
Canal Basin
Brideswell

Jake looked from the list to the map in front of him and back again, his heart thudding. This had to be more than coincidence. The sites mentioned in the Psi File stories were the same as the places he had photographed, the places he had just marked. They corresponded exactly. He sat back in his chair as another thought occurred to him, sweat breaking out on his forehead and upper lip.

That kid, Wendy Richardson, she had disappeared near Stoke's Weir.

A photo flashed into his mind, sharp in every detail. A splash of pink against Matt Black and Hookers Green. An item of clothing caught in iron spikes which ran like teeth across the mouth of a tunnel just down-stream from there. What had the child been wearing when she disappeared? Jake remembered from the description: a pink cardigan. Jake stood up, a numb feeling spreading through his legs, making them shake.

"Can I help you?" The young woman at Local Studies Enquiries looked up into serious blue eyes, magnified by glasses. "Oh, it's you." She smiled, recognizing him from earlier. "Do you need any more maps? You know where the drawers are…"

"It's not that…" Jake pushed his glasses up his nose and looked at the paper in his hand. He was holding it tight, creasing the bottom edge. "I wondered if you could help me with something else?"

"If I can. What do you want to know?"

"Tell me…" Jake cleared his throat. The hand with the paper shook slightly. "How do you find out abut missing persons and unsolved disappearances in and around the city?"

"Going back how long?" She swung round on her chair, turning to the computer console at her side.

"I'm not sure exactly." Jake readjusted his glasses again. "But quite a long time."

"Well, you can go through the crime statistics, and we've got the local papers on microfilm – dating back to the twenties. But it could take you quite a while."

"I don't mind that."

"We close early today."

"Oh, right."

Jake had forgotten about that, but he didn't go away. He stayed looking down at her until she took him over to the microfilm bank. He would find out what he could in the time allowed.

14

The police search of Brideswell Pool was looking less and less promising, so Cassie and Fraser went back to the playground, the place where the search had started.

"Anything turned up yet?" Cassie asked one of the young officers standing around. She had not been able to get much out of them before. She smiled now, hoping this one might be more communicative.

The policeman shook his head. He had taken his uniform jacket off. His blue shirt was navy with sweat: front, back, and under the armpits.

"Nah, not a sign." He scratched at his stubbled cheek with a thumbnail; he'd been on duty all night and was working on his own time now. "It's as if the earth had opened up and swallowed her again. No one's seen anything else since last night around nine to half-past. She was seen by some kids who were playing here, and also by a man walking his dog."

"Are you sure it was her?"

"The description fits. Girl, about six or seven years old. Long blonde hair. Yellow T-shirt, green leggings. Dirty, dishevelled. In some distress. That's why she was noticed."

"There's a bit of a gap, though," Fraser put in. "Time-wise, I mean. It's well over a week since…"

"I know," the policeman cut in, "but she was a cute-looking kid. Someone could have taken her, been keeping her. They don't always top 'em, you know. It could be a kidnapping. There's that many derelict sites round here: flats, warehouses, factories, houses" – he counted them off – "you could hide a regiment and no one'd notice. Plus there's that many weird people about…" He paused. "They reckon she was with a young lad."

"Really?" Cassie looked at him sharply. "I didn't know that."

"Well, it's not for general consumption until we can get an accurate description, so keep it under your hat. The old bloke with a dog saw this little kid with an older lad. The boy was dragging her along and she seemed reluctant to go with him. They went past here," he indicated the playground, "and over towards Brideswell. The old guy reckoned it might be her brother, but something about it didn't seem right to him."

"Why didn't he do anything?" Fraser asked. "When he saw them, I mean."

"He was going to, when he saw a big mob of other youngsters. They seemed to come from nowhere, he said. Scared him, I guess." The young policeman grinned. "I'm not surprised. Scare me, some of the kids you get round here. Anyway, he couldn't be sure it was Wendy. They were at a distance, and the light was fading, so he did the sensible thing, went home and phoned us instead of getting stuck in himself. There were some other kids in the playground." He looked around. "We've managed to locate most of them now. We've got officers with them, trying to get a better description of the lad, but some of the kids are pretty little, so it's slow going."

"Little? How little?"

"Six or seven, about the age of the girl who's missing. Some even younger…"

Cassie frowned. "It's a wonder they were out on their own at that time."

The young officer gave a laugh, harsh but not unkind.

"Look around you." He gestured towards the ring-road and the looming high rises. "This ain't Seymour Grove." He grinned as he saw he'd scored a hit by naming the white middle-class area where Cassie lived. "Dads and Mums at the pub or the club. Lots from one-parent families. Kids roaming around all over the place, all times of the day or night. It's a wonder more don't go missing. Sorry," he passed a hand over his eyes, "that was a bit insensitive. Like I said, she was seen with a kid. A lad about nine or ten, could have been older, definitely not younger. He was wearing jeans, and some kind of fleecy zip-up jacket, red, possibly maroon in colour, oh, and Nike trainers." He grinned again and shook his head, as if to say, "kids these days". "None of them can give us his hair colour, but they all agree he had Nikes on. One of them even named the model. Black and white Air-something. Are you all right, son?"

"Yeah," Fraser managed to mutter.

113

He leant against the wall, flushing fire hot and then drenched deathly cold again. Sweat sheened his face. His heart was bungy-jumping about inside him, plunging down to his stomach and then up to his throat again, squeezing the air out of his lungs, leaving him gasping.

"I have asthma." He took out his inhaler and shook it. "Excuse me."

He turned away, releasing the cartridge into his mouth. He hated doing this in public, hated the display of weakness, but he had to if he was ever going to breathe again.

"OK now?" the young policeman enquired, concerned, as Fraser turned back to them.

"I'll be fine." Fraser managed a weak smile.

"Well," he looked at his watch, "I better get off now. I'm on again at six."

"Hope you find her."

"So do I."

The policeman bit his lip and looked over to the bunched police cars, the dog-handler vans, the parties still out searching. He did not have to say anything; you could tell what he was thinking. Hope had sprung up again at this new sighting, given the investigation fresh impetus, but it could easily turn out to be nothing. Fraser was right. The longer it went on, the less hope there was of finding her. Alive.

"Are you sure you're all right?" Cassie asked when they were out of earshot.

"Of course I am!" Fraser shook her arm away. "Stop fussing, will you?"

He nearly said, "You sound like my mother," but

checked himself. His mother didn't care that much. She couldn't care less if he lived or died.

"It's just," Cassie went on in the face of his silence, "it's just you went so pale when he was talking about the boy who was seen with the little girl." She dropped her voice, even though they were well away from any police activity. "I thought, I mean, back then – it *looked* like you knew the person he was describing."

"Don't be ridiculous! How could I?"

"I don't know." Cassie pulled him round to face her. "But you do, don't you?"

"Maybe."

He dipped his head, unable to look at her. He had meant to brazen it out, on no account was he going to tell her, but he felt tired, drained, he could not lie, not with her deep blue eyes searching his. He no longer knew why he wanted to, he was no longer certain of anything.

"Well?" Cassie persisted. "Who is it?"

"It's Billy," he said at last, "that's who it is."

"It can't be!" It was her turn to deny what she was hearing. "He always wears black. He doesn't have clothes like that."

"He does now."

"How do you know?"

"Because I gave them to him. Last night. Before you picked me up."

"What do you mean? Are they your clothes?"

"Not exactly."

"I don't understand."

Fraser closed his eyes. "They belonged to Duncan, my brother. Clearer now?"

"But you said—" Cassie began, and then stopped.

"You do have a brother, then?"

"*Did. Did* have a brother," Fraser corrected, still with his eyes closed. "It is necessary to speak of Duncan in the past tense."

"What happened to him?" Cassie asked quietly, sensing that this was it, this was the thing he'd been hiding from her. Then she added, "You don't have to tell me if you don't want to."

"No. It's not that. I want to. I didn't. But I do now. I – I just can't seem to find the words to tell it. He," Fraser paused, "he was killed. It was – it was—" He still couldn't say, *It was an accident*. "He died, that's all."

"How?"

"He was—" Fraser cleared his throat, the words seemed to stick there like burrs. "We were climbing. He had a fall."

"When did it happen?"

"A couple of years ago. When I was fifteen."

"How old was he?"

"He – he was eleven."

"And you gave his clothes to Billy?"

"Yes. They were up in the loft, not doing anything, so…" Fraser gestured with his hands; there was no need for further explanation.

"And the clothes were the same as the ones that policeman described back there?"

"Yes. You've got it exactly."

"We have to go back!" Cassie caught his arm. "We have to tell them."

"No." Fraser shook his head. "I might be wrong. I don't want to be the one who sets the police on to him. The kid's got enough problems."

"But what if you're right?"

Cassie's eyes, intense, almost purple now, searched his.

"If I am, I know where he will have taken her. I know where he goes, where he'll be. There's a disused tower block. That's where I found him."

Cassie turned round. "Which one is it?"

"That one, I think." Fraser pointed towards the skyline. "You can tell from here that the windows are boarded up."

"OK. Let's go and see."

"Sorry, Miss." The policeman put a hand up to stop Cassie. "You can't go further than this."

The whole forecourt area of the flats had been cordoned off.

"Why not?" Fraser asked.

"It's a dangerous building, for a start. No access, so you'd be trespassing. But it's not that." He indicated the striped tape fluttering round the doorway. "It could be a crime scene. They've found something in the basement."

15

The remains discovered in the basement were not those of a child. The body was that of an old man, probably a derelict, a tramp who had broken in to find shelter, and his death had not been recent. There was an item to this effect on the local news, but certain details were not released to the public. Death was more than likely due to natural causes, but this would be difficult to establish. Substantial parts of the corpse were missing. This could be down to the attention of dogs, cats even, or urban foxes, but neither the police doctor nor the pathologist had seen anything like it before. It reminded one police officer of kill sites he'd seen on a Safari holiday in Africa, but he kept his opinion to himself. His boss would find that unacceptable; put it down to an overactive imagination. Such a thing was not possible, not here, in an urban basement in the middle of a British city.

This news item was small. The bulk of the bulletin

was given over to the continuing search for the little girl. Cassie and Fraser watched it together in her living-room. A police spokesperson summarized progress so far. Her statement was followed by another distressed appeal from the child's parents. Renewed hope showed on faces puffy with grief, eyes ringed from lack of sleep, prematurely aged by two weeks of thinking the worst. What if they were all grasping at straws? What if it wasn't Wendy after all? What if she was dead anyway, and all this new hope was false? Cassie turned the TV off; she just couldn't bear to think about it any more.

Fraser stayed for something to eat, and showed no enthusiasm for going home. It was getting late. Cassie's mother asked if he'd like to stay the night. He could have Jill's room since she was back at university. Fraser accepted gratefully. He did not fancy leaving this warm, lively household to make his lonely way back to a darkened house.

Later, when her brothers were in bed and her mum and dad had gone out leaving them to babysit, Fraser and Cassie had a chance to talk. Normally he'd have been dreading this, normally he would have been out of there, but tonight felt different. He wanted to talk about it, wanted to tell her about Duncan and what a great kid he'd been, so when she asked he was ready.

He told her about their life together, the places they'd lived, the games they played. He left nothing out; included the fights and arguments which he always won because he was bigger and stronger. They did not fight often, so luckily those times were few and were far outnumbered by the others, the good times they had spent together.

"Like I said, he was a great kid. Wicked sense of humour, a good laugh. It was like being with your mate, not your little brother, you know?"

Cassie nodded, then she said quietly, "So what happened?"

Fraser sat forward, rocking on the edge of his seat, hands locked round his knees. This bit was going to be far more difficult. Still, he'd made up his mind to tell her; she might as well know all of it.

He told her about the climbing trip.

"Duncan was made up. It was to be his first real climb, away from the novice faces. He had all the gear; Dad bought it for him. We were camping up in the Cairngorms; we still lived in Scotland then. Duncan loved that, too. He was so excited..." Fraser's voice trailed off as though he could see his dead brother standing in front of him, laughing, talking non-stop. "It was my job to check the gear, and I thought I had, I really thought I had, but..."

The phone rang, but Cassie left it, letting the answerphone deal with the call, as Fraser told her, in fits and starts, stopping every so often, describing the scene that he'd lived so many times over, in nightmares, sleeping and waking: the unlocking karibiner, the capsizing knot, the final sickening fall.

"But it wasn't your fault!"

"Whose was it then?"

"Nobody's. It was an accident!"

He looked at her, without answering, his half-smile twisting and bitter, his face bleak.

"You have to believe that, Fraser!" Cassie insisted, pushing her hands through her short blonde hair, appalled that he should take the burden of something so terrible all on himself. "What about your mum and dad?"

"What about them?"

"Surely they wouldn't want you to blame yourself?"

Fraser shrugged. "Dad blames himself as much as me, but I don't come off scot-free. Mum just said, 'It's beyond blame', and withdrew into herself." She was there still, locked in by booze and pills from the doctor; anything to kill the pain inside her. "And that's it," Fraser said after a moment. "Dad's out working all the time now. He's a sales rep for InterLect." Cassie recognized the name of a multi-national electronic firm which had recently relocated to their area. "He's on the road from one week's end to the next. He used to work in the office, but he changed his job specially so he doesn't need to be at home…"

With us. Fraser didn't say it in so many words; he didn't have to. The pain on his face said it for him. Cassie would not ask to know more about how he survived within the black hole that the death of his brother had created at the centre of his family life. Fraser was proud, not given to easy confidences. He turned away from her and stared down at the carpet, his long dark hair falling forward. Maybe he was crying, maybe he wasn't, but it had cost him a lot to say this much.

"Come here," Cassie murmured, and put her arm round him.

She drew him to her until his head was leaning on her shoulder. Her feelings towards him were changing, shifting to allow in a new respect. Then he looked up at her, green eyes deep with unshed tears, and in the time it takes to blink, she was ready to give him anything. The tricks he'd played receded into meaningless japes. The bet he'd had with Todd and Warren turned from a rankling insult to a silly boys' joke. Somewhere the phone was ringing again, but Cassie ignored it.

"Come here," she repeated, and her mouth met his.

Fraser lay between crisp, clean cotton, hands behind his head, thinking. He could not remember the last time his own bed had been changed; the sheets on that were limp and filthy, so this was real luxury. Jill's room still kept her presence, even though she was away at university. Her books spilled from overstuffed bookcases; ranks of cuddly toys stared at him, their blank button-eyes making him feel uncomfortable as he got undressed. Her dressing table was a mess of cosmetics and perfumes; the walls were covered in pop posters, some of the groups and gig dates dwindling into history.

Judging by their rooms, the two sisters were quite different. Cassie's room lacked all this girly chaos. It was uncluttered and tidy to the point of obsessiveness. Furniture was kept to a minimum and was entirely functional. Her walls carried art prints and film posters held in clip frames. Her dressing table was clear except for a bottle of CK and a metal tool kit which held her make-up. A few silver cased items; as much, but no more, than she needed.

Fraser stared up at her sister's purple ceiling. Cassie's was painted grey, or mushroom, or something. Her room was kind of like her, really. Understated, unshowy, but absolutely sure of itself. He turned over, burrowing his head into the soft pillow, waiting for sleep to come to him. She might appear cold and serious, aloof and distant from other people, but this was a guise to hide her true nature. Underneath she was warm, passionate even, liable to feel things strongly and deeply.

Fraser closed his eyes, captured by the novelty of feeling something for someone other than himself. Despite his good looks and attractive personality, Fraser had never had a proper girlfriend. He'd been with a lot of girls, but they were casual encounters; the idea of a steady relationship did not appeal. He found most girls boring. After a while, they wanted to run his life for him, or they thought he was weird and were unable to see where he was coming from. Apart from that, he had a horror of letting anyone get close, get under the skin, because that would mean caring about them. Caring about people was dangerous because anything could happen to them, and quite often did.

But Cassie was different. He was prepared to take the risk with her. She was not like any other girl. He lay drifting towards sleep, thinking about tomorrow. He would get to spend the whole day with her. The family were off to a theme park somewhere and he was invited. A regular family outing. A week ago, he'd have run a mile at the thought; now he was looking forward to it. Telling Cassie about Duncan had freed him to feel again. What could be dangerous about that?

Fraser's sleep was deep and dreamless, containing no echoes from the past, or warnings about the future. No hint that his feelings for Cassie would take him into far more danger than anything he could possibly imagine.

16

Jake tried to contact Cassie over the weekend, but all he got was a machine asking him to leave a message. He gave up eventually; he didn't cope well with answerphones. He'd even thought of phoning Fraser, but the other boy was not in the book and he didn't know his number. Anyway, his theory that there might be come connection between the Psi File sites and missing persons was just that: a theory. The library had closed before he'd really had time to research the missing-person angle. There was more to do. It would have to wait for Monday.

He dropped his little sister off and went straight to the library. He was there on the steps when the librarian unlocked the door.

"Hello," she said. "You're bright and early. School project, is it?"

"Kind of."

Jake pushed past her and went to the Local Reference section. He took a pad and propelling pencil out of his bag and settled down, breathing in the dry, musty smell of the old books and leather-bound volumes in the Records room. He removed his glasses and rubbed his eyes, thinking about where to start on his research; then for a while, sat lost in thought, eyelids beginning to droop. The day had hardly started, but he was tired already. He had not slept well. Thinking through his theory had kept him awake, and when he did doze off, he was woken by what he now called the *tunnel dream*. It was the same dream he'd first had two weeks ago. The one that made him get up at dawn and take the photographs.

He still could not remember specific images or forms, but the dream was full of threat and fear – not for himself, but for somebody else. All he could recall when he woke in panic, his mouth open, a silent screaming choking his throat, was a darkness that would not leave, that swallowed him back as soon as he closed his eyes, and the echoing drip of falling water. This was so real that some nights he had to get up to check all the taps in the house. He put the light on, willing himself to wake as soon as the dream began, not allowing sleep to come again. He'd read somewhere that that was what you had to do: stop the nightmare from forming.

He took up where he had left off on Saturday and spent most of the morning going back through the newspaper archives, noting down the names of people reported missing and the places they had last been seen. The list was long. It went back over decades. He had been shocked by the sheer number of people who appeared to have vanished from the city. Another surprise was that so many of the missing were children. That seemed odd.

Jake was not the only one to have noticed that. The newspapers reported periodic panics and talk of serial killers, but these fears had all eventually died down. The list went back to the beginning of the century while the last child had disappeared two weeks ago. No living thing could be responsible for that and all the others. No one person could operate over such a time span. So, if it could not possibly be down to any one person, to any man or woman, just exactly what were they dealing with?

Along with bursts of acute intuition and sudden quirks of insight, another of Jake's qualities was sheer persistence. His research had been thorough and painstaking. Now came the time to put it all together. "Show and tell," he muttered to himself and his hand trembled slightly as he shuffled the papers next to each other: Psi File list, missing persons, tunnel sites. The cross-referencing was perfect.

Some of the names were different – children have their own names for places – some had been updated: the Odeon Cinema, for example, used to be Howe's Theatre, the Lower Precinct had been the Old Market, and Fieldgate Lanes Shopping Mall had been built on an area just known as Fieldgate. That did not matter. The names might differ, but he was looking at the same places. Each one checked:

The Old Bridge: Becky Smith, aged 8, last seen 12/10/1967 playing near bridge.
Stoke's Pool: badly decomposed body found 1957, never identified.
(Stoke's Weir/Wendy Richardson, Jake added in pencil.)
Black Spinney: mining accident, 1929.

126

Runghills Copse: Tommy Haynes, aged 8, last seen 10/4/1979 playing on BMX.

Bishop's Clump: Angie Squires, aged 9, last seen 4/7/1956 when she wandered away from family picnic.

Odeon Cinema: Eve Driscoll, attended evening performance "Gone With The Wind", 1942 – never seen again.

Old Sun Rise (pub): tramp found badly mutilated in outhouse, 26/12/62.

Fieldgate Lanes (Shopping Mall): Joe Amos, aged 4, 21/11/1996, wandered off while out shopping.

Lower Precinct (Old Market): Brenda Chambers, aged 7, 14/2/1993, disappeared while shopping with her mum.

Jake put down: *St Martin's playground: Wendy R sighting.*

He added: *Burton House*, the disused block of flats where the police had found the remains of the tramp.

Then he wrote: *Brideswell*.

His pencil hovered, threatening to rub this out. Nothing had occurred there, as far as he knew, but he resisted the temptation to get busy with the eraser. Nothing had happened there yet, but adding it to the list seemed like the right thing to do.

So far, except for the last, every place on the Psi File list was associated with missing people, and these places were all associated with tunnels and underground entrances. He had photographs. This was potentially a massive story. For him, for *Orbit*, for Cassie. It would make the local papers easily, maybe even the national dailies, but it was not that which made his mouth dry and his skin grow clammy.

As he looked at the facts, a sense of foreboding threatened to overwhelm him. The gooseflesh came creeping back and with it the vile taste of his nightmares welled in his throat, dark green and slimy, like swallowed pond water. The fear which haunted his dreams was back – not for himself, but for somebody else. Maybe it was reading about all these other kids disappearing, but his anxiety was focusing away from the story and on to his sister, Amy. He had this terrible feeling that something bad was going to happen to her.

He gathered all his material together. He would take the evidence to Cassie and then go and meet his little sister. Maybe that would quell the fear gnawing away like a rat in his stomach; maybe that would put his mind at rest.

The sun had disappeared, the sky was overcast, but it was still hot, humid and oppressive. Jake's red hair was dark with sweat, his shirt sticking to him, as he pulled up outside Campbell Roberts School. He removed his cycle helmet, slipped through reception, and went up the stairs to the *Orbit* office.

He had hoped to find Cassie alone but Fraser was with her. Jake stood at the door seeing how they were with each other: sitting close, heads touching, his hand on her shoulder. He noticed the way they were talking, laughing softly, murmuring low, even though they were alone. All this told him something was different. Something had happened between them. Something more than had happened before. Jake could guess what it was. He did not have to be told.

The papers crumpled in his hand. Suddenly the story

128

seemed pathetic. She wasn't going to be interested. He debated whether to go, just sneak away and leave them to it, taking his theory with him. But he did not do that. He stepped forward, clearing his throat, rustling the sheaf of notes. Cassie turned round, blue eyes cloudy, pushing her silvery pale hair back from her forehead. Her face was slightly flushed, a pink bloom heightening her colour. She blinked slowly and looked at him as if she had never seen him before, as if she was waking from a dream.

"Hi, Jake. Where have you been? Mrs Weatherall's been looking for you," she added before he could answer, "there's been a call from the Juniors."

"What about?"

"She wouldn't say. But she was pretty agitated. Wanted to contact you urgently. She'd tried your home and there was no one there. It sounded kind of important."

Jake stared, reluctant to let her words sink in. The school could only have one reason for wanting to contact him. Something *had* happened to Amy. Papers fell from his hand and scattered round him on the floor. The nightmares he thought were finished were just about to begin.

17

"Jake! Jake!" Cassie called after him, worried by the sick, scared look on his face. "Hang on! I'd better go after him." She pulled away from Fraser's restraining hand. "He looked upset."

"Do you want me to come with you?"

"No." Cassie shook her head. Jake did not like Fraser and would not take kindly to his presence. "I'll go on my own. I'll just make sure he's OK." She stood up. "You stay here. I'll be back in a minute."

Fraser shrugged and let her go. He turned to the stories he'd been reading for inclusion in the next edition. There had been a fresh influx following their latest appeal for readers' own experiences so there was plenty to be getting on with. He picked one from the pile. It looked like a girl's handwriting. He checked the name at the bottom: Helen G. 7.RB. Then he began to read: *My gran told me that, when she was a little girl, her mum said to her, "You should never, never go to the woods..."*

It was only a page long. Fraser read to the end carefully, and for the time it took, he even stopped thinking about Cassie. What the girl had written was important. He folded the single sheet of paper carefully and put it in his inside pocket. He needed to look into it. The bell rang for home time. He debated whether to go off and see about this by himself, but he decided to find Cassie first and tell her about what he intended to do. He smiled. He was definitely changing: a couple of days ago, he would never have dreamt of consulting anybody else.

By the time Cassie got down to the ground floor, Jake was gone.

"It's his sister," Mrs Weatherall explained. "We received a call. She went home at lunchtime, to get something apparently, and didn't return for afternoon school…"

The school secretary carried on with her explanation, but she was talking to the air. Cassie left as fast as Jake. She shook her head. These young people. They didn't even have the courtesy to wait for the end of a sentence.

Cassie ran out into the drive and looked round. She didn't see him, but that didn't matter, she knew where he'd be going. She set off for the junior school.

It wasn't far. The two schools were next to each other. Home time was approaching. Mothers were already gathering, ready to greet their offspring and accompany them home. Something about the way they were grouped, talking together in little huddles, the way they kept an iron-fisted grip on accompanying toddlers, confirmed for Cassie that something had happened. She didn't need to see the police car pulled up outside the main doors.

"Excuse me, have you seen a boy…?" she asked a tall woman with a buggy.

"A kiddie's gone," the woman carried on talking to the cluster around her, ignoring Cassie's enquiry, "another one."

"It's the little Saunders girl," her friend added.

"She's in our Tara's class," someone gasped, clutching her four-year-old more tightly, as if going missing might be catching. "How do you know it's her?"

"Just seen her brother ride up to school."

Cassie leaned against the fence and waited for Jake to emerge. The woman had answered the question she had been trying to ask.

Cassie waited a long time. The noisy stream of children going home reduced to ones and twos and the staff were leaving before Jake came out. He was with a policewoman; she had her arm round him. He was shaking his head vehemently, arguing with her about something. Finally, he shrugged her off and went to pick up his bike from where it had been abandoned, slewed at the side of the front entrance.

He rode out of the gates at top speed, straight past Cassie without even seeing her, and on into the road. There was a sickening squeal of brakes, followed by shouting. Jake lay tangled in the frame of his bike, glaring up at a driver swearing down at him.

Suddenly strong arms were hauling him upright.

"Yeah? And what's that sign say?" A loud voice answered the driver for Jake. "Are you blind, or something? This is a school entrance!"

The driver pulled away, still muttering expletives.

"And you!" Fraser gave him the finger. "I can't stand guys like that, think they're everything. Are you all right, mate? He was right about one thing," he added, dusting Jake down while Cassie held the bicycle, "you ride around like that and you are liable to get yourself killed."

Jake looked up at the other boy, eyeing him suspiciously.

"What are you doing here?"

"I came looking for Cassie. Wasn't hard to figure out where she'd gone to. She came after you."

"What's happening, Jake?" Cassie asked. "What did the police say?"

"They said, they said" – Jake shook his head as if the words were flies buzzing around him – "not to worry. That it was early days. She'll probably turn up right as rain. To go home and wait."

It was clear from Jake's face that he did not share the official police optimism. His voice cracked and his face contracted in spasms as though bolts of pain were shooting through him.

"I don't believe them," his words were a whisper, almost inaudible, "and I can't sit around at home doing nothing. It would drive me crazy."

"What were you planning on doing?" Fraser asked.

"I was going to ride around. Look for her myself."

"I don't think that's a good idea." Fraser looked at Cassie, who had tightened her grip on the handlebars of Jake's bicycle. "Not in the state you're in." He nodded towards the skid-marks in the road. "You might have an accident or something."

Jake looked away. He did not say anything. He didn't

have to. They both knew what he was thinking. Ending up under the wheels of a car would be preferable to living with what might have happened to Amy.

"It's, it's my fault, you see," Jake said after a moment. "She left her clarinet at home. She had a lesson this afternoon, so she went back at lunchtime to get it. It's my fault she forgot it. We were in a rush this morning, I was hurrying her…"

He paused again, as if trying to recollect just why he had been in such a panic to get out. He had to go somewhere. Down the library, that was it. He had completely forgotten his obsession with the city's missing children. It all came back to him, names and facts rushed back to his consciousness, booming and barking in his head. Now his sister had joined them. It seemed like some sick cosmic joke.

"Anyway," he spoke on as if in a dream, as if the words coming out of his mouth did not quite belong to him. "Anyway – she forgot her clarinet and went home for it. Another kid saw her on the way back. She was cutting across the common, heading for the woods. There were some other kids up there, playing that game. We saw them the other day, you know? The seven steps?"

"The ones with Billy?" Cassie frowned. "Do you think she might have joined them? Have the police spoken to them?"

"They said they didn't see her."

"What about Billy?" Fraser asked, his eyes suddenly sharp with interest.

Jake shook his head. "They say he went off and the police can't find him. No one knows where he is. Anyway," he gave a long shuddering sigh, "I don't reckon she'd do that. I think she was just planning to take the short cut. It's the way we sometimes go, but I've told her and told her, she knows – only with me, not on her own, never, never…" He looked away, squeezing his eyes shut, trying to prevent the tears that were rising. "She never goes that way on her own. She doesn't like the woods, thinks they're creepy. She must have been that scared of being late…"

Jake stared down at the ground, trying to get a hold on himself, afraid to show his emotions, particularly in front of Fraser. Fraser could well take the piss, like Todd and Warren, like the other boys.

"It's OK." He felt a hand on his back and the arm of someone taller than him went around his shoulders. "It's all right, mate. Believe me, I know how you're feeling. Don't give up, though. We'll find her. Don't you worry."

Jake looked up at Fraser's green eyes, smiling down at him, full of concern and sympathy.

"But how?"

"First off, I suggest you and Cassie go back over the route you usually take…"

"The police are already out searching the woods and everything…"

"Yes, but you know your way exactly and they might miss something. There might be places they wouldn't look."

"Yeah." Jake nodded. There were places in the woods, places he knew about from his researching…

"What about you?" Cassie asked Fraser. "Aren't you coming with us?"

"No. I've got some business to attend to. I'll catch you later."

"Fraser! Wait!" Cassie called, but Fraser spun away from them.

It would take too long to explain now, but he had to find Billy as quickly as possible. There was not a minute to waste.

Fraser set off at a loping trot, weighing the options. He had a pretty good idea where Billy might be, but he needed some gear before he went there. He thought about going home, but Mum might be conscious enough to start asking questions, and Dad might be there. He was due back tonight from another stint on the road. There was a place on the way that could supply his needs.

He turned into a small hardware store in the centre of a little row of shops and came out stuffing various purchases into his pockets. A heavy-duty halogen torch with spare long-life batteries, a length of nylon rope, and a thin-bladed, rubber-handled axe. He was not quite sure why he needed that but had seen it up on a wall display and it looked like it might come in handy.

He resumed his easy jogging pace, his feet keeping time to a song running through his head. It was a rhyme he remembered from childhood. A clapping game the girls used to play in the village where he lived then:

My mother told me I never *should*,
Play with the gypsies in the *wood*,
    If I did, she would say,
    Naughty girl to disobey.

That's all he could remember, but the words sounded over and over like an ominous jingle.

The song had come to him as a sinister accompaniment to the story for the "Stranger than Fiction" section, the one from Helen G, the story which started: *My gran told me that, when she was a little girl, her mum said "You should never, never go to the woods..."* and went on like this:

...she meant the ones round our school, because one time a little girl did *disappear.*

The little girl belonged to the big house – the one that's now our school – except it wasn't a school then, of course, some rich man owned it. The one whose picture is in the foyer. Anyway, the rich man who owned the house doted on the little girl, because she was his only daughter and his wife had died having her, and when she disappeared he searched everywhere, round and through the whole area, but there was no sign of her.

He (the man) blamed his son, the little girl's brother, because he had been out in the woods playing with her. He treated the boy very cruel, beating him and locking him up for hours in a little room in the dark, he had the windows blocked up specially. My gran's mum knew all this because her sister worked at the big house as a servant. All the servants thought it was a shame and a scandal but there was nothing they could do about it. Jobs were hard to get in them days, Gran says, and if they said anything they would lose their position. They tried to do what they could for the boy but the old man never forgave him, not till his dying day. Cursed him from his deathbed, so the story goes. Said he'd never find rest or peace until his sister was found.

But the little girl was never found. Her name was Amelia. The boy's name was Frederick William. He

*went on to become F W Campbell Roberts. He didn't
have children of his own, that's why he left in his will
that the house should be made into a school. He was
very rich and owned all kinds of factories and
engineering works in the town, but my gran says he was
never a happy man. Her auntie stayed working there
right up until he died. He got a bit strange as the years
went on, didn't go out or see any one. There was
whispers that he didn't die a natural death, that he
killed himself, but that was all hushed up. He was a
good employer and the servants were loyal to him. They
called him "Mr William". Sometimes, Gran's auntie
told her, when the house was quiet, you could hear his
sister calling to him. The servants knew it was her sister
because she always called him Billy.*

This story had made the hairs rise on the back of
Fraser's neck. He had to get to the bottom of this. The
name check was too much of a coincidence. Billy was no
ordinary boy, that much had been clear from the very
beginning, but Fraser had noticed other things about
him. The things he knew, even the way he spoke.
Sometimes he sounded like any other kid. Other times
he sounded old-fashioned, as though he'd lived a long
time. But Billy was solid. Fraser had touched him,
grabbed him by the shoulder. He might be thin, all bone
and skin, but he was real, flesh and blood, nevertheless.
And yet, and yet...

Thoughts rattled and ricocheted, pinballing round in
Fraser's head, bouncing off questions, nudging
speculations, but he was still nowhere near any kind of
acceptable explanation. For that he would have to find

Billy. Jake's sister disappearing made it even more imperative. Billy was the kid seen near the playground with that other little girl, he was sure of it. What if he had been involved in abducting her? What if he was connected this time, too? Even if he was not, it was likely that he knew about it. He'd been in the woods at around the same time Amy was last sighted. It was a sure bet Billy would not talk to the police, even if they could find him, so it was up to Fraser to get it out of him.

Fraser ran on, leaping traffic barriers, by-passing shoppers and school kids going home. He kept to the main roads, he still didn't know the area well enough to take short cuts and didn't want to waste time getting lost. Cassie's local knowledge would have helped, but he had to do this on his own. She would be safe with Jake. There would be police and all sorts in the woods, so nothing bad could happen there, could it?

18

Jake dragged his bike up off the ground and prepared to mount it.

"What are you doing?" Cassie stared at him. "I can't keep up with a bike!"

"You don't have to." Jake straddled the crossbar. "You can come with me. Get up on the saddle. Ride behind me."

"But, Jake…" Cassie looked dubious. Riding two on a bike was dangerous. "How are we going to follow the route? Look for clues? We might miss something—"

"We haven't got time for that!" Jake shook his head impatiently.

"Where are we going?"

"Runghills Copse. Now get on!"

Cassie sat on the saddle, long legs dangling either side of the back wheel, while Jake pumped the pedals. It was hard-going at first, the bike seesawing alarmingly back and forth, until they began to pick up speed. Cassie held on tight to Jake, gripping him round the waist. His skinniness disguised considerable sinewy strength and the gradient was in their favour. They swept down the steady curve of the suburban street, flying along the long, looping road.

Eventually the houses thinned, giving way to scrubby hawthorn bushes and stretches of fencing. Jake braked and brought the bike to a jolting halt.

"Come on," he said, throwing the machine behind a hedge, not even bothering to lock it.

Cassie followed him at a run, vaulting the stile that led on to the common. Paths zig-zagged through tawny clumps of seeding grass. Jake set off along a narrow track which branched left, leading towards a wooded rise which marked the edge of Runghills Copse. Cassie ran after him, trying to match his pace, but the long sapping incline made it tough going. It was hot and humid. The air all around was motionless and the temperature seemed to be rising – it was like running in a sauna. The sky above was overcast, dulling from pewter to gun-metal grey. It looked as though there was a storm coming.

They were approaching the trees, Cassie noted with relief. Once they were up there the slope would flatten out and inside the woods, maybe it would be that bit cooler. But it was worse, if anything. Hot stagnant air seemed to be trapped; the leaves drooped, limp as rags. Flies and midges swarmed in thick bands of black, dancing mist, plastering themselves to Cassie's sweating skin, getting up her nose and in her mouth. Jake ran at the same steady pace, oblivious of everything, but Cassie had to stop, even if it meant losing him. She just could not go on any more; she had to have a breather.

She leaned forward, hands on knees, spitting out flies, taking in great gulps of air, trying to ease the stitch knifing her side, while Jake disappeared round a bend in the track.

It was some moments before Cassie could hear anything above her own rasping breath, the thudding in her chest. When she did recover enough to straighten up, there was a silence, a stillness around her which did not seem quite natural. No birds sang, no animals moved; the only sound was human: the distant crash of men beating through undergrowth, calls from parties looking, like them, for any sign of Amy.

Cassie went on, slackening down from Jake's hectic pace. The ground inside Runghills Copse was uneven: hilly and hummocky, split with steep-sided fissures. The path they were following skirted the deep saucer-shaped depression at the centre. Normally boys on bikes swept up and down the nearly vertical slopes, but there was no one about now; no yells and shouts, everything was quiet. Cassie had time to look about her now, her eyes searching each side of the narrow path. That was why she saw it.

"Jake! Back here! Come quick!" she shouted up the track, and began a headlong descent, slipping and sliding her way through the undergrowth.

Tall nettles stung her bare arms and thick looping brambles grabbed at her legs, threatening to tear through her jeans, but she kept her eyes fixed on the flash of silver she had seen from above. It would probably turn out to be nothing, another piece of litter, a discarded can or chocolate wrapper, but there was something about it that had caught her eye and held it.

The object was right at the bottom of a long cleft in the side of the hill. Too thin and narrow to be called a valley, the stream running along the bottom had shrunk to a trickle in the recent dry spell. It was damp and slippery underfoot. Cassie jumped from one moss-covered stone to another to save her trainers and stop herself sinking into the mud.

"Come and play, come and play,
We're off to find the Seven Steps today..."

She stopped for a moment, thinking she could hear children's voices singing, a far-away silvery chant. She looked down at her feet and on towards the hillside. Further stones, big, rough hewn, but normally covered by water, led into dense foliage.

"One, two, three, four
Five, six, seven..."

"Cassie? What is it?"
Jake's voice, shouting from above, roused her and she looked away from the stones to the object which half-lay in the bushes. She reached over, pulling it free of the bramble suckers already beginning to wind themselves round it. The silver gleam that had attracted her attention came from twin metal clasps set in to black imitation leather. She had one just like it. A clarinet case.

Cassie held it gently, turning it round in her hands, cradling it against her body, reluctant to let Jake see what she had found. It was heavy. The clarinet must still be inside it. And there could be no mistake. *AMY P*

SAUNDERS read the peeling dynotape label on the back. Musical instruments were expensive. Jake and Amy came from a one-parent family. Amy was young, but she knew how many extras shifts her mum had to work to save for this. She would not lose it, or leave it, or put it anywhere unsafe. She would not be parted from it, not voluntarily.

Jake knew, too. The yell of anguish he let out when he saw what Cassie was hiding from him spread up and out, echoing away through the woods. Search parties stopped what they were doing and ran in his direction and tracker dogs started up barking and howling in sympathy.

Jake stood at the bottom of the slope, his heart gripped, squeezed by fear. It held him so tightly that his skin went clammy, his face felt numb beneath its sheen of sweat. He looked up the narrow defile where they were standing, where Cassie had found the clarinet. A line of flat stones, shaggy with moss, slippery with weed, lay in the muddy stream-bed and led towards the hillside in front of them. Thin stripling trees fought their way through a rioting tangle of old man's beard, bryony and bramble, but Jake knew that underneath this curtain of vegetation lay a crumbling bank of earth and stone, and in this there were caves. The stream itself issued from one of these subterranean outlets.

Jake set off at a run, splashing through the stream.

"Stop!" a voice came from above him.

Jake looked up for a moment and then went on, ignoring the policeman crashing down the slope towards him.

"I said, *stop!*" the man shouted again. "Andy! Phil! Get to him!"

Two other policemen appeared from the other side of the gully.

"What's your hurry, son?" one of them asked, as he came up in front, cutting Jake off.

"There are caves under there!"

"OK, OK. Steady on." The policeman looked down at him, arms folded. The stripes on his shirt showed him to be a sergeant. "Now, what's going on?"

"We found this." Jake showed him the clarinet case. "It belongs to my sister, Amy. Amy Saunders – the one who's missing!"

"Where did you find it?"

"Back there." Jake pointed towards where Cassie was standing. "But there's caves under the overhang, and—"

Jake made to break away, but the sergeant pulled him back.

"I said, steady on! Andy," he turned to one of his colleagues, "go and see, will you?"

The two men exchanged looks. It might be a crime scene; there was no telling what they might find. Not for a kid to see, particularly not the brother.

Cassie came over to join Jake as Andy splashed up stream and disappeared through the overlying undergrowth.

"What kind of shoes did she have on?" he shouted back.

"Trainers," Jake replied. "Size 12."

"There's kids' footprints." The man called from under the overhang. "Two sets. One pretty small, one a little bit bigger. Both sets fresh. Look like trainers, the bigger look like Nikes, my son's got some just like… Hang on. That's weird… The kid's right. There's kind of a cave back here. I'm going in to take a look."

145

His voice faded momentarily and then came back from further up the overhang.

"It makes a kind of a tunnel. The prints go on a little way and then disappear in this small cave-like entrance."

"Disappear?"

"They get lost in a mess of other tracks. All kind of small…"

"Maybe there were a bunch of them," the sergeant suggested, "using the place as a den or something?"

The other policeman frowned. "Maybe. But how many kids these days run around bare foot?"

"What do you mean?"

"There's two sets of trainers and then these other ones, all scrunged around but they look like they were made by bare feet. Like tracks on the beach. Hang on, I've found something…"

The policeman returned to them, holding up a sweatshirt. It had Minnie Mouse on the front. The motif was mud-covered, trampled almost out of recognition.

"Know it?"

Jake nodded. "She was wearing it this morning."

Jake turned away, too full to say any more. The sweatshirt belonged to Amy. Her auntie had bought it for her on a visit to America. He had insisted that she take it when they left for school. She had complained that it was too hot and had tied it round her waist.

"It was inside the small cave-area."

"Let's have a look a minute."

The sergeant took the sweatshirt from his colleague. The fabric was torn at the shoulder and down one arm. There were plenty of brambles and thorns about, perhaps the girl had slipped and torn it. On the other hand, sweatshirts were made of tough material and the edges of the tears were clean, as if they had been slashed with a sharp instrument. But what could have done that in a pattern of four? A rake? A fork? A claw? His mouth compressed, and his brow furrowed even more.

"How deep is the cave?"

"I don't know. It goes back quite a way. Can't really see without a torch."

"She might have gone in, though?"

"Yeah. Could have…"

"Right, we better get on to it. Bag that garment and get it off to Forensics. Get a cast of the prints. And we'll have to search the cave system."

"You'll have a problem." The second policeman frowned. "The cave narrows to not much more than a fissure – a crack maybe this wide…" He measured with his hands less than a metre. "A small kid might squeeze through, or a dog, but not a grown man. We'd have to enlarge it quite considerably, and that'd take time…"

"Better get going, then, hadn't we?"

The sergeant unclipped his radio and spoke into it. He seemed to have quite forgotten Jake and Cassie standing next to him.

"You've done a good job," he said, when he finally noticed them again. "Thanks for your help, but leave it to us now. We'll find her, don't worry. You go on home. Any news, good or bad, we'll let you know."

"Jake! Jake! Where are you going?"

They were nearing the crown of the woods. Jake was heading up the hill fast; Cassie was having trouble keeping up again. The atmosphere was getting even more oppressive and, as they stepped out on to the rock-strewn space which marked the summit, the clouds seemed to bear down and the air felt saturated like a warm sodden towel.

This was the highest point for miles around, and on a good day you could see a long way. But this was not a good day. In one direction, the city sprawled: a mesh of roads and mass of buildings lying, blurred and indistinct, under a fine heat-haze which was fast being turned by choking exhaust fumes into a foul brown-tinged smog. In the other direction, countryside spread out in a drying patchwork, intermingled green and tawny as various crops ripened by the recent sun moved towards harvest. Except the sun was not shining. Tractors crawled the fields as farmers worked against time to cut their grass and bring in the silage in the face of the threatening storm. Purple clouds the colour of bruises were massing and building. Overhead, the sky was darkening by the minute.

"Look! Just look!"

Cassie followed Jake's pointing finger. On the horizon, lightning flickered, first in one place, then another, each crooked flash followed by a time-lapsed roll of distant thunder.

"We can shelter in school. Wait until it's over…" She looked down towards the buildings nestling below the line of trees.

Jake shook his head vehemently. "I don't mean that! Don't you see?"

Cassie frowned at him, puzzled.

"No, I don't. You've lost me."

"Under here," Jake stamped on the bare earth, "there

148

is a cave system. The ground is honeycombed with tunnels, some manmade, from mining and quarrying, others natural…"

"So?" Cassie's frown deepened; she still did not follow.

"So this. See there, and there, and there…" He swept his arm round. Grey veils of rain were sweeping towards them, blotting out the circling horizon. "It is already raining. Heavily. Soon it will be raining here. There is a storm coming. Where will the water go?"

"Into the streams and rivers…"

"And, round here, a lot of those flow underground. It's really quite simple. Surplus water pours off the land, particularly now after this dry spell, and drains down and down. The earth acts like a sponge, soaking it up. What happens when it becomes saturated?"

"I see…" Cassie was catching on now; geography had never been her strongest subject. "All the tunnels fill up."

"Exactly. Anything alive down there would drown." Jake turned towards the school. "I can't risk that happening."

"What are you going to do?"

"If Amy's in there, I'm going after her. I'm going to use the school's caving equipment. I know where it's kept."

"What about the police?"

"What about them? You heard what he said. They would have to break a way in and they have to get a team together. It could take hours."

"But how are you going to get past them? They're swarming about all over the place."

"Sometimes we use the system for practice. There are other ways in."

"But Jake," Cassie held his arm, "aren't you going to tell them at least?"

"Of course not," he said, simply. "If I did that they would stop me."

"Jake, wait," her grip on him tightened, "how do you know she's down there?"

"I don't, but she isn't anywhere else, as far as we can tell. They found her sweatshirt – what more proof do you need?"

"But – even if she is – how are you going to find her?"

"If she's down there, I'll find her."

"How can you be so sure?"

"I just know."

"But you can't do it on your own…"

Cassie bit her lip. She wished Fraser was here. He'd go with Jake in a minute, be there for him, look after him. Jake could get lost down there, or fall, get injured. And if he was right about the storm, he was just as likely to get trapped by the rising water as his sister. What he planned to do was highly dangerous. If he went alone, it could be fatal.

"You can't," she said finally. "It's crazy. You can't go down there alone. Please, Jake…"

Jake looked at her, his pale eyes cold behind his glasses, as distant and implacable as the winter sea. Cassie knew she was powerless to dissuade him. The only way to stop him now would be by physical restraint.

"You come with me, then."

"I can't…"

Jake shrugged. "Make your mind up." He took her arm in his strong grip, forcing her hand off his wrist. "Either come with me, or let me go."

150

19

Fraser looked up at the derelict block of flats. The windows stared back at him like rows of eyes, empty and patched.

He went to the boarded up doors and slit the blue and white police scene-of-crime tape. Just as he did so, the first rain hit. Drops as big as pennies splashed down the splintered wood. Fraser pushed the doors open and let himself into the entrance hall. Some of the trash had been cleared, presumably by the police. Fraser stood in the middle of what remained, perfectly still, listening carefully. Outside the wind was getting up, the rain was intensifying, hitting the doors with some force now, banging the loose plywood, but inside all was quiet. Except... Except for the tiniest little scuffling, scraping noise, and that was coming from under the floor.

Fraser headed for the door marked BASEMENT. Billy was the key to it all and this was his hang-out, his hiding place. If anyone knew where Jake's sister was, he did. Fraser kicked open the basement door and switched on his torch. Any sign of reluctance, let alone refusal on Billy's part, and he would ring the boy's scrawny little neck for him.

The terrible gagging smell had begun to disperse now that its source had been removed, but still a hint remained, clinging in the nose, hitting the palate like gone-off fish paste.

"Billy! Are you down here? Billy, I want to talk to you! Billy! Answer me!"

"Shh."

Fraser had no idea how he appeared, but suddenly the boy was there by his side.

"Shh," he whispered again, a finger held to his lips. "Be quiet or they'll hear you."

Billy was wearing Duncan's clothes, the clothes Fraser had given him. The bright garments seemed out of place on his skeletal frame. His deep-set eyes peered up, black and shadowed, from under the peak of a baseball cap too big for his bony skull. He looked like a scarecrow.

"Who? Who will?" Fraser grabbed Billy by the throat. "Don't play games with me. I'm sick of all this weird stuff." The boy's neck felt unpleasant, kind of loose and squishy and unnaturally cold and clammy, like chicken skin, but Fraser's grip tightened until he was almost choking him. "Tell me!" he hissed. "Where's Jake's sister, and that other little girl?" He shook the boy backwards and forwards like a rag doll. "You know, don't you? You better tell me or, I swear, I'll…"

"All right, all right," Billy gasped out, "but let me go!"

"OK. But don't run away." Fraser unclenched his

fingers, transferring his hold to Billy's shoulder. "Who's this 'them' you keep talking about?"

Billy's eyes flickered towards the scratch marks on the back of the door. Deep scores indented the surface, exposing bright metal. Fraser's eyes widened. Who, or what, could make marks like that?

"Come with me." Billy jerked his head towards the steps. "Stay close and I'll tell you."

Billy went down into the basement. Fraser followed after him, playing the torch round the area below. A patch in the corner was cordoned off, that was where the tramp must have been. The rest of the basement was filled with boxes, rotting pallets, general debris. Billy was heading towards an uneven break in the crumbling concrete of the far wall. It looked like a giant rat hole. He beckoned to Fraser.

"Through here."

They were in some kind of service tunnel put there to carry cables and pipes to the flats above. Billy moved fast, working along the cramped space with ease, but for Fraser it was a tight fit. He had to go crab-style.

After thirty metres or so, Billy ducked into another basement area. This one was empty. Billy crossed the dusty floor and stepped through another hole in the wall.

"We're under the shops now," he said, as Fraser looked around. "Welcome to home-sweet-home."

Fraser shone his torch over and through the space. In one corner there was a makeshift bed, a stack of pallets spread with filthy old sleeping bags. By the side of it lay the carrier bag that had held Duncan's clothes.

"You got a light?"

Fraser reached in his pocket for his zippo.

Billy took it and lit a little rank of nub-end candles set out on the top of an orange box.

"There," he said, as a yellow glow filled the room. "Nice and cosy."

"Terrific." Fraser turned off his torch. "But I didn't come down here to start playing house." He advanced towards the boy. "What exactly is going on? And you better not bullshit me, Billy."

"All right. But you won't believe it…"

"Try me."

Billy perched crosslegged on the bed. Fraser sat on the end of it, staring into the leaping candlelight, as the younger boy began his story.

It certainly was fantastic. If anyone but Billy had told him, he would not have believed it. But Fraser had been told things, had seen things, knew things, which put this boy outside the normal world, beyond the limits of what is credible. This alone gave Billy's tale authenticity, apart from the fact that it also contained its own weird and sinister logic.

It was a tale stretching back for almost a century; a tale of love and betrayal, of a father's curse and a debt claimed from beyond the grave. Billy told of a boy and his sister. The boy was twelve, the age Fraser judged Billy to be now. His sister was younger. Eight years old. Four years difference. Just like there had been between him and Duncan. The brother and sister lived in a grand house, set in its own grounds, a house that had since been turned into a school. They were educated at home, by governess and tutor, and they spent a lot of time together, either in the nursery at the top of the house, or out in the woods that grew all around.

The little girl, Amelia, was beautiful, with blue eyes and rosy cheeks, blonde curls and rosebud lips. She looked just like one of her dolls. She was the darling of everyone, particularly her father. Their Mama had died giving birth to her; his daughter was all he had left of his adored wife. He doted on her, declaring her to be the spitting image of her mother, who in her day had been a very great beauty. She was the favourite of others, too: servants, nurses, tutors, governesses. All of them thought she was absolutely perfect. Only her brother knew different. There was a wild streak in his adorable little sister which, as she grew older, became twisted and cruel.

She lived a double life. In the house, or when adults were about, she was sweet and charming, obedient and biddable, "a lovely little thing", "no trouble at all", but at other times, out in the woods, or when no one was around, she showed a different side.

She loved animals and was allowed to keep a variety of small pets: little birds in pretty cages, linnets and canaries, kittens and baby rabbits. She would fuss over them like a little mother. Except none of them lasted very long. She would be found weeping over some pathetic little corpse or other: someone had left a catch undone, a cage open and one of the cats, or one of the dogs, had dispatched the inmate. The unfortunate victims were buried with great solemnity in the pet cemetery by the ornamental lake, and everyone in the house felt sad for her on these occasions. They, like her brother, who helped at the little ceremonies, were moved by her obvious unhappiness and hurried to supply her with a replacement. But, all too often, these little creatures would go the way of their predecessors. Everyone declared it "most unfortunate".

None of them ever guessed at the real reason for this high rate of pet mortality; only the animals knew. The many cats who lived in and around the outhouses would not go anywhere near her. The dogs her father kept shied away or growled deep in their throats whenever she came close.

Even her brother had no idea, he never suspected. Until one day, when he was out in the woods, he heard a high-pitched yowling cry, the unmistakable call of an animal in great distress. He ran towards the sound, thinking it was a rabbit caught in a trap. Miners from the colliery owned by his father came into the woods sometimes and set snares along the rabbit runs.

He followed the sound and suddenly came upon his sister standing at the centre of a clearing. She was holding a stick, beating and beating at something. She threw the stick away as soon as she saw him approach and turned to him, all bewildered innocence, making no attempt to hide what lay at her feet. It was a cat, or it had been. It was still warm, but so pulped and mutilated it was hard at first to see what kind of animal it was. The skull was crushed, the back broken, fur matted and caked with blood, belly split and insides spilling out.

His sister ran to him, throwing her arms round him, sobbing into his shoulder. She was so glad he had come! Now he was here, they could give the poor little thing a proper burial! She had found it like this, the victim of some awful attack by some terrible creature. A fox, maybe, or one of the colliers' lurcher dogs.

Terrible creature indeed. Her brother held her away

from him. The stick she had thrown away was clotted with fur and blood. She had hit so hard, again and again, that her face was spattered and streaked, as were her legs and dress. Above all, seconds before she saw him, he had seen her eyes, blank and shiny, staring upwards in a blind ecstasy of pleasure. Whatever she said now, he knew. She had done it, and she enjoyed it. Killing for killing's sake.

He left her, running from her as if she was some kind of devil. She ran after him, crying piteously, pleading with him to wait for her, pleading to be forgiven, promising never to do it again, if only he would help her, help her to be better. His legs were longer, he quickly outstripped her. Her voice faded, and faded, and then suddenly, abruptly, it stopped altogether.

There was no sign of her now. No sound in the woods at all. He paused to look around. The area he had been running through, the place he had led her into, was riddled with abandoned mine workings. Now they are all capped and fenced off, ringed round with signs, but then they were just yawning holes in the ground, opening up with no warning. A sliver of intuitive knowledge, thin as a knife blade, bit into his consciousness. He suddenly knew that she had stepped through the sparse layer of disguising grass and undergrowth and fallen into one of these gaping pits, some of which were hundreds of feet deep.

He went back home without his sister. When the day wore away to evening and Amelia failed to return, he said he had not been with her, had not seen her, had no idea where she could be. The search for Amelia went on for days, months, years. His father combed the woods,

157

the fields, the town, and then the whole country for any sign, any news of his beloved daughter, but no trace was ever found.

His father never recovered from the loss. He became more and more withdrawn, more and more obsessive. All he cared about was making money and finding Amelia. Always a hard employer, he became ruthless now, wringing profits from his factories and mines with little regard for his workers' safety and lives. He treated his son with particular cruelty. Perhaps he thought the boy somehow responsible for his sister's disappearance, or perhaps it was just the loss of his favourite, but the beatings and harsh treatment went on until the boy was a man himself. He cursed him every day, he cursed him from his deathbed.

The torment did not stop with the death of his father and the onset of adulthood; if anything it got worse. Because, every now and then, Amelia would come back to him. In the night. When he was alone. When he was walking in the woods. In some ways she was horribly changed, in others still the same. She was lonely, she said, she wanted for company. She would be happy in the new place where she was living if only she had someone, something to play with. And he wanted her to be happy, didn't he?

And so he gave her what she wanted, to keep her at bay, keep her away. Pets at first, puppies and kittens, cats and dogs. But then she demanded playmates, children her own age, or younger, to keep her company. It was still lonely, she explained, she wanted for playmates in this new world she had found, so many feet underground. So, God forgive him, he gave her those, too.

"This boy. The brother," Fraser said when Billy had finished, "that's you."

Billy nodded.

"But I don't see – all this happened a long, long time ago. So how can you possibly be here, like this?"

Billy's face seemed to wizen in the flicker of the candlelight, the skin stretching and wrinkling paper-thin, and the eyes seemed impossibly old. Fraser understood. Billy had lived all his life in thrall to a ghost child, until he became one himself.

"Why go on doing these things?" Fraser shook his head. He couldn't understand. "When you know it's wrong? I mean, how could you?"

"Amelia is too powerful for me. Always was, probably. And it's not just her. There's a whole brood of them. They become like her, you see, the ones she takes, the ones I give her..."

Fraser remembered one of the stories he had read, the one Cassie had dismissed as too utterly fantastic.

"You mean, like vampire children?"

"Not vampires in the strictest sense." Billy thought for a while, and then he said, "I don't think there is a name for what they are."

"Where do they live?"

Billy looked at him, incredulous. "Haven't you been listening? They live here. Under the city."

"Can't you – can't you stop them?"

The boy slowly shook his head. "I've tried, many times, and each one ends in failure, just serves to make her stronger. I need help. I need you to help me. It's all getting too much. She's getting greedy, she needs to feed them. I'm tired. I don't want to do it any more..."

159

Billy's voice tailed off. His tiny face crumpled like an old paper bag and he sat rocking backwards and forwards on the bed. His eyes were squeezed shut, the grey skin around them crinkled and pouched, as if he was trying to shut out the dreadful things he had done, the terrible scenes he had witnessed. Fraser stared at him, trying to make sense of what the boy had just said. It seemed as though Billy genuinely wanted to change, but he had been doing his sister's bidding for so many years. Why change now?

"What about that little girl," Fraser asked, suspiciously. "Wendy Richardson? You were seen with her."

"I was trying to get her away from them, don't you see?" Billy's opened his eyes, looking at Fraser in desperate appeal. "But the child was too heavy for me to carry and too weak to go far. They caught us. I can't do it on my own. You've got to help me..."

"What about Jake's sister?" Fraser asked, looking hard at him. "You didn't, you didn't help them to get her?"

Billy didn't reply, just shuddered, burying his face in his hands.

"How could you do that?" Fraser recoiled from him, appalled.

"My sister, Amelia, she can make me do things, make me suffer..." Billy's voice was low, muffled by his fingers. "You wouldn't understand."

"And Jake?"

"What about him?"

"What if he goes after his sister?"

"He won't. They took her underground."

"What if he does?" Fraser insisted. Jake knew about caving, and he would do anything for Amy. Just as Fraser would have done for Duncan. Give his life. No problem. "He will go after her." Fraser was certain. He shivered. That thought chilled him more than any of the other stuff.

Billy shrugged. "Then they will get him."

"But he's big – almost grown-up."

Billy shrugged again. "It's not just little kids they take. There's a lot of them. They hunt in a pack, like dogs. They would have taken you, if I hadn't stopped them."

"When?"

"Outside the old hospital. You were cut. They could smell the blood. Even a kid as big as Jake wouldn't stand a chance…"

What about Cassie? If Jake went down, Cassie would be with him. She would not allow him to go on his own. What might they have in store for her? The thought exploded into Fraser's consciousness, leaving him frozen and speechless. Suddenly he found it hard to breathe. His chest was tightening, his breath coming in shallow gasps. He fumbled in his pocket for his inhaler.

"Excuse me," he said, releasing the canister into his mouth.

The relief was immediate. He could face Billy now. He stared at him, green eyes like chips of glass. He was just as bad as his sister, worse in some ways, acting like some kind of judas goat, leading the innocent to a hideous fate. Fraser shuddered, his breathing thickening; spasms of fear, mixed with anger and revulsion shook him. If Billy had done anything, *anything* to put Cassie in danger, he'd tear him apart, right here, right now. Fraser shivered again; he had to get a hold of himself. He was wheezing like he had a lungful of kitten fur. He took another jolt from his inhaler. Attacking Billy wouldn't do any good. He was the only one who knew where they were. Without Billy he would never find them.

"OK." Fraser frowned, hands locked together, knuckles white with tension. "What do you want me to do? Where do we go from here?"

Billy jumped down off the pallets and extinguished the candles with the palm of his hand.

"Follow me." He led Fraser towards another hole in the wall. "Turn off the torch. Try and do without it."

"How will I see?"

"Your eyes will get used to the dark," Billy said, stepping through the gap.

"Where does this lead?" Fraser asked as he followed him.

"Into the sewers. Keep quiet and stay close. Where we are going is very dangerous."

20

Cassie adjusted the webbing belt round her waist, taking it in a notch or two. The flat battery-pack clipped to the back was heavy and kept pulling it down. The light on her helmet was attached and ready but Jake said not to turn it on in order to conserve the batteries. They would use natural light for as long as possible. Given the heat of the day outside, Cassie had thought that the big boots and waterproof suits they were wearing would be impossibly hot and uncomfortable, but down here the temperature was the same, winter or summer.

They were at the beginning of a cave system. Part natural and part manmade, it extended for miles, right under the city and out the other side. Jake was quite aware of the risk he was about to take, and the dangers that they might face, and had taken care to equip them properly with the right clothes, ropes and harness. He also had a backpack containing drinks and high-energy snacks. He had strapped on a wrist compass and round his neck he wore a flat waterproof case containing an ordnance survey map, diagrams of the sewage system he had obtained from the city planning office as part of his Underworlds project, and a plan of the cave system as far as it had been mapped.

He was examining this with a small hand-torch. He had another light in his pack, a powerful halogen lamp, but he would not be using that except in emergencies.

"We'll go this way," he indicated to Cassie. "It will take us through the area where Amy might have entered the system."

He set off down the cave. Soon the circle of light that marked the entrance dwindled to nothing, and as they turned the first corner, Jake told Cassie to turn on her lamp. Cassie was surprised at how much light they gave. Perhaps it would not be so bad, Cassie reflected, swallowing down the first nagging taste of claustrophobia. The tunnels were tall enough to walk in, the ceiling arched high above their heads and the floor was dry. Their boots crunched on pebbles and the bare rock surface. Jake stopped every now and then to consult his compass, mark the wall with chalk, or check their progress on the map. Cassie began to trust in the fact he knew what he was doing and pushed her fears resolutely back. She refused to think about what would happen if the lamps went out; about the yards of rock, the hundreds of tons of earth weighing down on top of them. Instead she concentrated on Amy, finding her and getting her back to safety.

"The system we are in now is a natural formation, created eons ago by percolating water..."

Cassie had said nothing to him, but Jake was aware of

her terror of enclosed spaces. Her face was chalk-white under her helmet, she had not spoken since they started and her footsteps were dragging and uncertain in the darkness. Jake could sense her fear and the effort she was making to overcome it. Talking would help her take her mind off her situation, help her to overcome her dread. It also stopped him thinking about what might be happening to his sister.

"Along there," he continued, indicating an entrance they were passing, "it's manmade, the result of quarrying. They dug deep, seeking a particular kind of hard rock suitable for building. Further on we will probably find evidence of mining."

He went on, explaining features in the rock, showing her the glistening formations of mineral deposits. His words were helping. Cassie found herself relaxing; she was beginning to find it interesting rather than a terrifying ordeal. Suddenly he stopped. The cave ahead split, running off in two different directions. Jake shone his light along each one, and then back the way they had come.

"As near as I can calculate it," he said, "the larger of the tunnels leads to where Amy would have entered the system." Jake paused. Only a slight hesitation, a gruffness in his voice when he mentioned her name, betrayed his fear for his sister. He must not give way to anxiety; he must banish it from his mind. Just like in caving or rock-climbing, he had to focus on the job in hand, tackle difficult tasks one bit at a time. He flashed his torch up and down the tunnels. "That way leads to where we came in, so she must have gone down there."

"How do you know?"

"I don't. Not for sure... Hang on."

He ventured in a little way and came back holding something. He opened his fist to show her what he had found. There, in the middle of his palm, was a Minnie Mouse hair slide.

"This is hers." His fingers closed around it. "She definitely went that way. Come on."

He led the way, quickening the pace now. Every so often he stopped to call his sister. He banged on the wall with a metal cup. "Sound travels a long way down here," he explained as the hollow clang echoed on and back.

"Knock twice if you can hear me," he shouted and put his ear to the rock face.

He did this many times with no response whatsoever. Then, just at the point where the cave entered a wider, squarer tunnel, Jake beckoned Cassie over. He rapped with the cup and pointed to the rock face. Cassie put her ear against it. There it was, faint and unmistakable: two raps back. Cassie turned to Jake, sharing his excitement. He rapped again and they both listened together. The reply came after a few seconds delay, and with it something else. They both heard it and took a step backwards, instinctively moving closer together. Far, far, distant, drifting like mist back down the tunnel, came an indistinct mutter, like the voices of many children whispering together. The murmur was mixed with chuckling laughter, mocking and sinister, enough to bring on shivers and chill the blood. It had to be a trick of the ears, they told each other, the trickle of a stream not so far discovered. What other explanation could there possibly be for such a sound down here?

166

21

Whoever said sewers don't smell, that it's really quite nice down there, was lying. Fraser took one whiff, took one look at the churning, turbid browny-yellow scum moving slowly below him, and immediately lost his lunch. He stood on the platform retching helplessly, each intake of breath making it worse, until he thought he was going to faint.

Billy grinned. "It's like the dark — you get used to it. After a bit you don't notice it. Try breathing through your mouth."

Fraser tried that, but the very air seemed heavy and thick; it could be swarming with lethal micro-organisms out to poison him. He'd rather get used to the smell.

"We don't have to go down there and wade about in it, do we?"

Fraser gazed down at the evil bubbling mass; he was not at all sure he could handle that.

"No." Billy grinned again. "We can keep to the gantries

and walkways the sewer men use. We only have to follow the system for a bit; it's safer than other ways for this particular stretch. Just watch out for the rats, that's all."

How was it safer? Fraser was about to ask, but mention of rats made him look about. He was not particularly keen on rodents, but they did not bother him, not in the normal way of things. The ones he saw now gave him reason to re-think his position. There were eyes, like red pin-points, all around. He flicked his torch on, and immediately wished he hadn't. The creatures didn't even flinch back. They just continued to watch him, eyeing him incuriously, completely unafraid. Their fur was sleek and thick, they were the size of cats! Miniature poodles! The torch shook in his hands. Some had teeth as big as beavers', and naked, hairless tails the width and thickness of electrical cable.

"They won't hurt you," Billy said, "as long as you don't go near them."

"Good. That's good," Fraser replied, as one flopped off a ledge into the filth below.

He hoped Billy was right. If he was wrong and the creatures decided to attack, the only way to fend them off would be with a double-barrelled shotgun.

"They're only found here anyway," Billy added. "They can live in this bit – that's why we are using it. Further in, there ain't any. They kind of die out." He laughed, not an entirely pleasant sound. "We better get a move on. There's worse than rats down here," he said, suddenly serious. "Much worse."

"How much worse?" Fraser asked.

"Worse than you can even imagine, and we don't want them to find us."

168

"Amelia's brood, you mean?"

Billy did not reply. He just shook his head and looked down the tunnel in front of them, his expression unreadable.

"No more talking," he said after a moment. "Come on. Let's go."

The tunnel Cassie and Jake were following was wide and high enough to stand up in. They trod on a spongy-wet splintering path of rotting sleepers, for this had once been part of a mine system dug long ago by men tunnelling like moles, following seams of coal. It suited Jake and Cassie's purposes; they had no way of knowing that, in Billy's experience, it was one of the tunnels best to be avoided. He would only use it out of dire necessity, and then with the greatest quietness and caution.

Jake and Cassie were not aware of this. They walked along, talking in normal voices, Jake telling her all he knew about the history of mining in this particular location.

The whole area was rich in minerals, much of it found on land owned by the Campbell Roberts family. Successive generations had fed off the wealth below the ground, sinking shafts to allow the freer exploitation of this valuable resource. These were greedy men, mean and grasping, with little thought for the safety of those who worked to make them wealthy, and mining is a dangerous business. There had been many accidents and explosions; over the years many miners had been killed.

In one notorious incident, back in the early part of this century, Colonel William Campbell Roberts, a man well-known for his callousness, had refused to fund the

169

recovery of the bodies of twelve miners trapped by a rock fall. Their remains had been left underground, the gallery where they had been working turned into their tomb. Miners are notoriously superstitious and stories sprang up quickly. Within a week or so, none of the miners would work anywhere near that particular gallery, declaring it to be haunted.

"Did this happen round here?" Cassie asked, not sure that she liked the sound of this.

"No." Jake shook his head. "It happened miles away, over the other side of the city."

Jake was pretty sure the accident had happened a long way from here, but underground direction is less of a certain thing and, in the telling, the true location of an incident often gets shifted.

"Anyway…" Jake continued; now that he had started, he might as well finish the story.

Belief in the haunted gallery was handed down from generation to generation, right up to the day the mine closed, early in the 1990s. Stories persisted of eerie cries for help coming from the tunnel depths, of knocking from behind the rock face, of scrabbling noises as though the trapped miners were trying to claw their way out by their bloody fingernails. Even the rat, the miner's curse and companion, had deserted that section…

"Rats!" Cassie's nose wrinkled. "I hadn't thought about them. Not that I'm bothered," she added quickly, "not that I've seen any about, either. Have you?"

"No. No, I haven't, come to think of it…"

As if on cue, the knocking started. It was different from the faint rapping they had heard before. There were two separate sounds, one ringing and regular as if made by a pick, the other more scraping and clinking, like a shovel.

"What's that?"

Cassie turned. Her ears seemed to move on her head. It felt as though slivers of ice were slipping down the back of her neck. The sound seemed to be coming from behind the smooth wall of the tunnel...

"I don't know..."

Jake went towards the rock face, putting his ear against it. He stepped back, white faced and shaking. There were noises from the other side of the rock. Not human exactly, more like the breathing and groaning of some great creature. Then the sound broke down to gnashing and snarling as of a number of creatures fighting among themselves. The nearest parallel Jake could make was feeding time in the lion enclosure. Whatever was behind there sounded hungry.

"Come on!" He grabbed Cassie's arm. "Let's get out of here!"

They fled forwards down the tunnel, the light from their helmets veering and weaving, illuminating now the floor, now the ceiling, as the knocking behind them started up again with renewed vigour.

"Not much further now," Billy whispered over his shoulder to Fraser, "just along here and—"

"Oh, no!" Fraser interrupted. "I'm not going down there. No way!"

He could see over the smaller boy's head. The gantry they were on stopped, marked off by an iron railing. There was a gap at the side where a ladder led to the channel beneath. The rest of the journey would have to be continued along a slippery brick path only inches above the turbulent flow of the city's filth.

"You'll have to," Billy insisted, swarming down the iron rungs. "The ledge is wide enough. Look straight ahead and just take it a bit at a time. It's not for all that far. Just take it slowly and carefully."

Fraser followed him down. The path was slick with slime; he set his feet down one at a time, relying on his climbing experience. He had a good head for heights and remembered a trick his father had taught him. The knack was to pretend that you were walking on a plank laid out on flat ground. This took away the anxiety and made it harder to fall. Fraser concentrated on that and staring straight ahead. He would rather fall off a mountain ledge than into that lot. This close, the smell was indescribable. The thick organic stench was laced with the reek of harsh corrosive chemicals. The surface of the stream was laced with vicious yellow and lurid green swirls which indicated some sort of spillage.

They went on in silent single file and, all the time, the flow below them was getting faster. Floating material spun past at an ever-increasing speed. The level was rising. It must be raining hard outside. The run-off drained down here from all the city streets. Soon it would be up to their shoes; they would be forced to wade. When that happened, they would no longer be able to see where to put their feet and the risk of falling in would be very great indeed.

Fraser was just about to call out when Billy stopped without his prompting. He frowned down at the channel. He, too, had noticed the quickening flow, but he had noticed something else. A sudden rippling surge, followed by another bigger one. He glanced up at the curved brick ceiling of the tunnel. Up in the world above, it must be raining very heavily. A storm, a cloudburst, breaking over the city. Which meant, which meant – he looked back at the stream, noting another surge, the biggest one yet. They were nearing a place where many storm drains and conduits converged, funnelling excess water from the city centre.

He stared back the way they had come. Even if they turned now, and ran for their lives, they would never regain the ladder in time. They could not outrace the tidal wave of filth heading their way. Billy could hear it roaring along the sides of the tunnel. In less than a minute it would hit, knocking them off this narrow ledge, sweeping on down the main channel, taking them with it.

There was one hope left. One slight chance of survival. "Up there! Quick!"

He pointed above Fraser's head to a small opening in the wall. It looked like a narrow doorway. Fraser gave the torch to Billy and jumped for the edge, but missed. He did not have to be told the danger they were in. He, too, could hear the dull roar of approaching water. The sound was magnified by the confined space and a breeze stirred the previously still and fetid atmosphere as the pressure of the oncoming wall of water squeezed the air in front of it. He tried again, catching on to the edge by his fingertips, but he could not keep his hold and again dropped back. This time he nearly lost his balance; his right foot slipped and he almost fell backward into the fast-flowing stream.

Gathering his strength for one last try, he jumped

again and this time felt rough stone under his hand. The stone was far older than the surrounding Victorian brick. Fraser gripped on to its grooved uneven surface and obtained enough of a purchase to run his feet up the slippery wall. He boosted his entire body upwards, and dived head first into the narrow gap.

The space was small; he had trouble turning round. He wriggled himself into the correct position and leaned out to Billy. The boy threw the torch up and then grabbed for Fraser's hand. He caught on, his trainers squeaking on the wet surface as he scrabbled frantically. Fraser pulled him in just in time. They lay side by side, panting, as the space in front of them became grey and opaque, a solid mass of moving water. There was no danger of it flooding into this high-sided chamber, but they wormed backwards as quickly as they could to avoid the risk of getting splashed.

Once the immediate danger was over, Fraser flashed the torch around. The tunnel they were now in was very different from the one that they had just left. Its dimensions were smaller, and it was constructed from the same stone as the ancient walls and buildings which Cassie had shown him the other day.

"I didn't want to come up here," Billy whispered in his ear, "I wanted to avoid this part but…" He looked back at the rushing water. "That way's impossible, so needs must." He paused. "You must make no sound, no sound at all, or you will alert them. Put the torch out."

"Who's 'them'?" Fraser asked. "Amelia's brood again?"

But Billy was already turning away, working his way forward along the uneven stone floor of the tunnel. So

174

far Fraser had shown himself to be brave and resourceful, but he was human and if he knew the full horror of what lay ahead of him, he might freeze, refuse to go on, and Billy needed him. Without Fraser he was doomed to fail.

"I want to know!" Fraser pulled him back. "Tell me!"

"Shh! Stop it!" Billy was beginning to panic. The slightest sound, the slightest stir in the air, might signal their trespass to the ancient presences which haunted this particular place. "They might hear you."

"Who *are* they?" Fraser insisted.

Billy looked round apprehensively. They did not have time to talk, and stopping here would be the worst place possible, but Fraser's forehead was creased and frowning, his mouth set in a stubborn line. He might not go forward without an explanation. Perhaps the roar of the water would drown their voices, perhaps not, but the look on Fraser's face told him it was a risk he would just have to take.

"We are under the oldest part of the city. It's all but disappeared from the surface, but down here," he indicated the old grey stone work above him, "it still exists…"

Billy's voice sank to an urgent whisper as he described a dark underworld filled with the ancient dead. Some rested peacefully, while others did not. All the evils that had ever been, all the city's sins were buried here. Those whose crimes in life were so great that they lived on after death. Murderers, criminals, suicides, buried in unhallowed ground, denied the rites of holy office. And others, buried in haste, victims of the plagues which had periodically ravaged the city. Whatever the reason, eternal rest had been denied to them. They had become foul wraiths, vile spectres, haunting the surface living, feeding off them, fuelling all the stories and speculation which Fraser had been collecting. Down here was where they lived; they were condemned to prowl the forgotten depths of the city, forever hungry for human kind, for the life they had left behind. They were dangerous beyond measure, to be avoided at all costs.

"So, if you see anything, hear anything," Billy concluded, "you must ignore it, just keep on going. They can only move within a small area, that which is enclosed by the ancient walls of the city. Once we are beyond those boundaries we pass outside their notice."

"But..." Fraser began to say, but Billy put his hand up to silence him.

"Enough. We have stayed too long already." He turned his back on Fraser and began to wriggle forward, moving with a stealth driven by fear. "Follow me and remember, *absolute silence*. If they catch you, death will be the least of your worries."

Fraser moved after him, pulling himself along by the elbows, easing his shoulders through the narrow confined space. Then Billy stopped. Fraser looked past him to where the tunnel halted abruptly and opened on to a shadowy chamber.

Light filtered in from somewhere above to show a stone flagged crypt with a high, vaulted ceiling. They would have to cross this space if they were to continue their journey. The circular room was lined with stone shelves. Upon each one Fraser could see vague shapes. Hairs stirred on the back of his neck and he fought down a shudder as he realized what they were. Human remains in different stages of decay. Skeletons showed through rotted linen. Bone poked through skin dried to cracked parchment. Thick cobwebs hung in ragged drapes, knitted across the narrow spaces like secondary shrouds. The air was foul with a peculiar sweetish musty smell that made the sewer stench seem healthy by comparison.

Billy knelt on all fours, watching. When there was no movement, no indication that any of these were in a state to detect their presence, he indicated to Fraser that it was safe to continue.

They moved with great stealth and care, taking enormous pains not to disturb any of the sleepers there. Nevertheless, they were only perhaps halfway across when a movement in the far corner set up a gossamer stirring among the cobwebs. Something rolled, dark and liquid, inside the bone-white rim of a deep eye-socket and peered out at them from under a fringe of green, decaying cloth.

This slight movement triggered one and then another; it was as if they were signalling to each other. Billy, alert to the tiniest change in the chamber, looked round fearfully. There was only a couple of yards to go to the squat archway which marked the exit, but already the figures on either side of it were moving. Suddenly the floor before them seemed yawning and enormous. What he had dreaded was about to happen.

Billy grabbed Fraser's hand, all efforts at caution abandoned.

"Run for it!" he hissed.

They sped over the space remaining, praying to reach the open doorway before bony arms, outstretching from either side, had time to meet across the middle.

22

Cassie and Jake ran on and on, only stopping in their headlong flight when they found themselves back in the natural cave system. There was silence here, no sinister knocking, or eerie chuckling, only the dripping of water. That seemed to be coming from everywhere, pouring down the walls, dropping from the roof into spreading pools. The water they were standing in was up to their knees.

"That thunder storm must have hit. It must be raining outside, and heavily, for the system to fill up as quickly as this."

"Where are we, do you think?"

Jake consulted his map.

"Well, I reckon that mine must be the old Clarion Colliery. It's the only one this side of the city. The top part's gone now. It's now B&Q and Safeways." He checked his wrist compass. "We're heading south west." He shone his torch along the black surface of the water. The level was rising, creeping up the sides of the tunnel, even as they looked at it. "Judging by the amount of run-off coming in here, I'd say we were nearing the city centre."

They ploughed on, but it was tough going. The roof above their heads was getting lower, and the water was getting deeper. It was up to their thighs now, and bitterly cold. The water had weedled its way through Cassie's waterproof leggings and was soaking down into her boots, seeping up the legs of her trousers – not a pleasant sensation. She looked ahead doubtfully. It seemed to her that, not too far forward from here, there was going to be a place where rock met water.

Jake stopped so suddenly Cassie nearly cannoned into him. As she had suspected, the next section of tunnel was flooded. Jake began to unbuckle his pack.

"Jake, what are you doing?"

He uncoiled a length of rope, tied one end on to his belt and gave the other one to Cassie.

"Hold on to this."

"Hang on, Jake!" Cassie's eyes were wide with terror. "Stop! You can't dive in there! You can't leave me alone out here!"

But it was too late. He had gone.

Cassie's worst nightmares were nothing to this. To be left alone, God knows how many feet underground, with the weight of all that rock and earth pressing down. The light from her lamp was just a sickly puny beam incapable of probing any distance into the darkness...

It was probably just moments since Jake had left, but the seconds stretched towards what seemed like eternity. Cassie stared, eyes wide and unblinking, all her attention fixed on the place where Jake had plunged in.

Thoughts raced and jostled in her head but nothing stirred the still, dark water.

What if the tunnel narrowed right down? What if he got wedged and couldn't work his way back? What if the tunnel went on and on, far beyond the point when the air in his lungs became exhausted? What would happen, then? He would drown in there; he could be drowning *now*. She would have to go in, try to rescue him. What if she, too, got trapped? Cassie fought to control her panic. She could not handle that.

But what was the alternative? To be left out here on her own? She would never be able to find the way out by herself. She would be condemned to wander for days, in the dark once the batteries went flat; no one would ever find her. Self-pity overwhelmed her, threatening to take away what little common sense she had left inside her.

"Jake…" Tears thickened her throat, her voice came out in a small sob. "How could you do this to me?"

Suddenly he was there, rising like a fish at her feet.

"It's only a couple of yards." Water sluiced down him as he stood in front of her. "Come on. It's easy."

"Maybe we ought to go back…"

"No." Jake looked at her, his pale face set and adamant. "The ground rises immediately after the tunnel and a bit further up there looks to be a ladder. We'll be out of the water in no time. And I found this." His fingers opened to show a small plastic figure. "I found it on the other side, floating on the surface."

Cassie studied the toy in the light from her helmet. The doll had yellow hair in a ponytail and purple-spotted dungarees; it was the kind little girls like to keep in their pockets. Jake held it cradled in his hand as if it were something infinitely precious. He turned it over, to show the back. There were his sister's initials APS. Amy had scratched them on herself. This was a warning not to turn back. It was a sign that they were heading in the right direction. Whatever was waiting for them, they had to go on.

Billy ran, with Fraser stumbling after him, through what seemed an endless maze of ancient, crumbling stone-built tunnels. Suddenly he stopped, putting a hand out to steady Fraser and a finger to his lips to indicate caution. Fraser had a brief sensation of the space he was in opening out, of air all around him. The cold stone smell seemed to change, lose some of its dampness, and then Billy flattened himself against the wall, pulling Fraser with him. Fraser could see nothing in the intense blackness but Billy's eyes were different. The low tunnel they were in had led them into an underground hall of cathedral proportions.

"Got to be careful here," Billy whispered in his ear.

They were in the most dangerous area of all.

Billy stood absolutely still. His ears seemed to move, to stir, so intently was he listening for any sound, any sign that their presence had been noted. When he was satisfied that all was quiet, he took Fraser's hand in his and indicated with a flick of his head that they should move forward. Absolute caution was needed. The things here, vile remnants of some impossibly corrupted monastic order, were steeped in evil and ancient malice.

They liked to play tricks. That was the worst part of it. They liked to play cat and mouse, although no mouse or rat, nothing alive, would survive within their dark boundary.

Billy paused, every now and again, and took up his intense listening stance. Fraser listened, too. At first, he could hear nothing. Then he picked up what sounded like a snuffling, or sniffling, followed by a slight skittering, which stopped when they stopped, and started up when they went on, like some sinister kind of "Grandmother's Footsteps".

The third or fourth time he risked a look round. What he saw froze the blood, made it impossible for him to continue, even though Billy was pulling at him more and more frantically. Fraser blinked, once, twice, and held his eyes open wide, trying to gather all possible sources of light. The darkness seemed to sway and flutter, first one way and then another. The black air itself seemed to be flowing over the ground towards him, moving of its own accord.

Billy glanced back to find his worst fears confirmed. His night-sight picked out one figure, then another, and another; a whole host of black swathed figures, ranged from wall to wall, advancing as one. Cowls hid faces long robbed of flesh, robes hung in folds round skeletal limbs. Bone ticked and scraped on stone as the creatures whispered towards them. They had no sight. Where their eyes should have been were just empty sockets. They hunted by scent, sensing the presence of warm human blood.

"Quick! Down here!"

Billy pulled him to the right and Fraser found himself in a passage branching away from the main chamber. There was a thin hiss of rage, as if from a predator cheated of its prey, but the Black Monks need not have concerned themselves. Billy slowed, his pace faltering. It was a dead end. There could be no escape. The tunnel was blocked off. The hissing sound increased, rising decibel by decibel, to a many-voiced banshee screech of triumph.

23

Cassie climbed on and on, legs aching, concentrating on the iron rungs in front of her. The corroded iron of the ladder flaked and crumbled wherever she grasped it. The brackets which attached it to the walls were almost eaten through. Cassie tried not to think about that, or how much further they had to go. She took Jake's advice not to look down and stared straight ahead instead, drawing satisfaction from the fact that this manmade structure was taking them up and out of the flooding water below.

Suddenly, just above her, Jake stopped. He grunted, legs braced against the upright supports of the ladder, and heaved, head and shoulders jammed up against a trap door. He heaved again, straining every muscle.

Red rust showered down into Cassie's face and the whole ladder lurched and shifted. The bracket next to her hand tore like paper. She bit back a cry. The wall in front of her eyes moved to the side. The ladder was pulling away.

Jake pushed one more time and the heavy weight above him began to give. He drove up, using his hands this time, and the flap banged over. Jake scrambled through, and then reached down to pull Cassie with him. The thrust of her heel sent the rusting ladder clattering down into the chasm below them. Whatever lay ahead, they could not go back that way even if they wanted to.

They were at the end of a long corridor. The lights from their helmets cut shafts through the murk to show light green paint peeling from wall and ceiling. The dirt of years lay clotted in corners, heaped in drifts across the floor. A fading notice proclaimed *All personnel must wear helmets at all times* and an enamel plaque, the corners nibbled away by damp and corrosion, proclaimed them to be at *Emergency Level Three*.

"This must be some kind of civil defence facility." Jake looked around, flashing his torch up at the notice. "Left from the war, or maybe after – to be used in the event of a nuclear attack."

"I know where we are!" Cassie exclaimed. "Under the town hall!"

"How do you know?" Jake glanced at her, curious.

"Mr Chetwin told us in history. The shelter was built during World War Two because of the air raids, and expanded out afterwards ready for World War Three. He didn't know for certain, because it was secret, but that's what he reckoned." She played her torch up and down the corridor. "Looks like he was right, though, doesn't it?"

They passed rooms with furniture still in them. Offices with filing cabinets ranged around the sides.

Desks still strewn with curling files and yellowing paper freighted with dust. Cassie half-expected to see a skeleton dressed in khaki, lying in one of the chairs, or face down on one of the tables, but they saw nothing like that. The effect was strange rather than ghostly, like stepping into an abandoned world, a time capsule.

"Which way?"

A second corridor branched to the right. They stood undecided, their torches swinging probes of light down the two dark tunnels, when the dusty silence was broken by a sound so everyday, so ordinary, that for a moment neither of them reacted. It was a telephone ringing. Clear and distinct. Not the subdued tone of a modern appliance but the full, rounded ring of an old Bakelite phone.

They both froze for a moment, and then Jake set off, back the way they had come, throwing open doors until he found the source of the sound. An old-fashioned telephone, shrouded in cobwebs, standing in dust inches thick on a desk which had not been touched for decades.

Cassie followed Jake into the room. *Brrrng! Brrrng! Brrrng!* In here the ringing was deafening. Cassie fought down an impulse to cover her ears. Jake's hand hovered for a moment over the big black receiver curved on its cradle. Then he snatched it up.

"Hello?" he said, trying to sound normal but his voice coming out in a small croak.

There was a click and the line went dead. He returned the receiver, sweat from his shaking hand leaving a slick palm print on its dusty surface. As soon as he put it down, the ringing started again, making both of them jump.

This time Cassie picked it up.

At first there was just the sound of the open line and then she heard giggling, stifled sniggering, like kids making a hoax call.

"Who's there?" she asked, her own voice also shaking and quavering.

The sniggering was no longer smothered, it redoubled, getting louder. Then behind it, Cassie heard another sound. A sharp cry of pain followed by sobbing, and a little voice said:

"I want Jake!"

24

Fraser and Billy had to run, even if they could not escape, neither wanted to turn and face what was coming up behind them.

The end of the tunnel had been sealed off with modern breeze blocks. Fraser felt hope leap up in his throat. Whoever had built the barrier had done a sloppy job. The grey concrete blocks had been thrown together, fat flanges of mortar oozed over the edges and corners. The sides did not fit snug to the walls. They had been built straight up so the curvature of the tunnel left a gap. Maybe there had been no time to do the job properly, or whoever had been sent to work down there felt no desire to linger. Whatever the reason they had left just enough space for someone to squeeze through to the other side.

There was plenty of space for Billy. The smaller boy was through and out like a rabbit down a hole, but for Fraser it was a different matter. The gap was only inches wide. He was too tall, too wide to get through it.

The hissing behind him had started up again; the creatures were near, picking up his scent, savouring the fear in it. The pace of pursuit slackened as the black shrouded figures re-grouped to move in for the kill. They were so close Fraser could feel the cold that surrounded them, smell the graveyard stench they carried with them.

They were not going to get him. Fuelled by adrenalin, he worked with fevered speed. Reaching into his pocket, he took out the stainless steel axe he had purchased in the hardware shop and hacked ferociously with the pick end of it. The mortar was spongy with damp, laid too thick, badly mixed. He managed to loosen one block and felt the others above and below it begin to give.

"Look out!" he yelled, and shoved with all his strength, his shoulder and back braced against the makeshift wall.

Billy leapt out of the way as the blocks began to tumble and suddenly Fraser was there, standing in front of him.

They were at the base of a concrete stairwell. Water stained the walls and puddled the floor; it smelt of urine, like all those places did, but Fraser had never been so happy to be anywhere in his whole life. The hissing had stopped. The black robed spectres were already withdrawing. The old city walls acted like a kind of time zone and they could not operate outside them. Fraser and Billy were beyond their territory.

Best to be on the safe side, though.

"Come on, Billy!" Fraser grabbed the thin iron handrail which led up to the surface. "Let's go!"

*   *   *

189

The wooden door at the top was padlocked from the outside. Fraser used the axe to hack a way through the lattice slats and then used the blade to lever the hasp. It came away with a rending crack and they were free, in the outside world again. They emerged from the base of one of the giant concrete struts which held up the ring-road circling the city.

It was still raining and the sky was dark, heavy with the promise of more. Fraser sucked in the cool wet air; it was polluted by fumes from the traffic but he didn't care. Cars hissed through the rain, their lights flashing like chains of stars. Fraser closed his eyes, thankful to be out in the open again. It was magic.

He wanted to go out under the sky, let the rain pour over him, cleanse away all the below-ground filth that had collected on him, but Billy pulled him back into the shadows.

"We have to stay here. It's not safe to go out yet."

"What?"

"They are watching."

"Where?" Fraser leaned out, scanning around, keen to get a first glimpse.

"Over there."

Billy pointed to a group of three or four sheltering under the opposite strut of the bridge.

Fraser shook his head. "I don't see anything. Just a bunch of kids."

"Are they, though?"

"Looks like it to me."

"Kids they may be, but they ain't ordinary. They can pass at night, or in this kind of half-light, but you'd never say that if you saw them in broad daylight, not that they are ever out at those times. You'd spot what was wrong with them straight away. Teeth too sharp, nails too long, clothes too dirty."

Billy stared in their direction and, as if alerted by his attention, one of the group opposite turned his head, and then they all did. Six pairs of eyes, pinprick red in the dim light, turned to stare at them. Their insolent gaze reminded Fraser of the fearless indifference shown by the rats he had encountered when they first entered the sewer.

Fraser turned to Billy. The boy was smiling. His white face seemed almost transparent, the lights of the cars travelling past seemed to go straight through. His eyes were black, as deep and fathomless as the darkness they had just left behind them. Fraser felt his chest tighten and automatically reached for his inhaler. All through the tunnels, he had never been so terrified, yet breathing had come easily. Now he felt as if a big hand was squeezing the life out of him. Because, just then, when Billy looked over to Amelia's sentinels, Fraser felt something, a kind of pulsing, like a signal passing between them.

"Are you all right?"

"Yes," Fraser managed to say.

"Good," Billy's small hand, skin webbed grey over skeleton bones, touched his arm. "Because we've got to move out."

"I thought you said it wasn't safe?"

Billy just shrugged. He was gazing past Fraser, away from the look outs, over to the garage across the other side of the ring-road.

"Places to go. Things to do." He looked up at Fraser and smiled. "Don't worry – it's all part of the plan."

25

Jake and Cassie came to a set of big steel doors, curved to the shape of the corridor. These were opened by metal bars, the kind you get on cinema exits, and led through to a different area altogether. The flaking painted walls gave way to chipped and dirty white ceramic tiles. Green watery light seeped in from outside through small grilles of thick, bulgy glass.

Cassie thought they might be under the disused hospital, the place where they picked up Fraser the other night, but she didn't say anything to Jake. The two of them were moving as quietly as ghosts now, navigating on instinct.

They could have easily become lost in the labyrinth of tunnels and heating ducts which underlay the old hospital, but for the strange marks on the walls and the tracks in the dirt of the floor. These could have been kids breaking in, but they did not think so. Kids did not make scratches like that. Kids wrote their names, made patterns, drew recognizable signs and symbols. These were just random markings deeply scored, like an animal might make. The tracks were too big for animal prints. The small foot marks were obviously human in shape, but what kid went barefoot? The toes looked elongated, with claws at the end of them. These tracks had been made by whatever had been on the end of the phone, by whatever had Amy.

The sets of tracks and prints, scuffed in the dust and dirt, led into what seemed to be a regular thoroughfare, a wide central corridor. Jake's hopes rose. Something told him Amy was close.

This route was barred by more big steel doors, like the ones they had come through before, with iron release bars. Jake held them lightly, his ear against the smooth metal. He sensed that it was very thick, blast-proof, bomb-proof, probably leading to some kind of shelter for the hospital to use in case of war or national emergency. There was something else. Faint sounds were coming from the other side: high shrieking cries, like the noise from a distant playground. Cassie went to speak, but he shook his head for quiet. There was definitely someone, something, on the other side.

He was going in. If Amy was there, then it was his job to get her out. He would do it, too, even if all the ghosts of the city were ranged against him. He pushed down the metal bars, first one, then the other. They went off like twin gun-shots. All sound stopped. You could hear a pin drop.

The doors led to a short passageway that opened out into a large room. Jake looked round, the beam from his helmet sweeping across what appeared to be empty space. There was no one here. The sound he'd heard must have been his ears playing tricks, he must have imagined it. He looked again, trying to see what kind of space they were in. The ceiling was low, the dimensions vague, the far sides lost in shadow, but Jake got the impression of size, at least as big as the gymnasium at school, maybe even the sports hall. The floor was covered, from one end to the other, in rat's-nest heaps of rags, paper, decomposing cardboard, mounds of clothing and goodness knows what else mouldering away. The septic, festering mess gave off a foul smell, a marsh gas mix of rot and decay.

The steel doors clanged. Jake whirled round, too late. They were shut flush, flat against each other. No handles on this side, no bars. Impossible to even slide a sheet of paper down the crack between them. Jake cursed. Their primary escape route gone. But how did they snap closed like that? There was nothing there, nothing at all. Only two more heaps of rags piled up either side in the space where the wall met the door.

He felt Cassie's hand clutch his, squeezing hard. He turned back to face the room and saw that they were not alone.

A walking, talking Edwardian doll was coming towards them. She seemed to glide on tiny feet encased in button boots of rotted kid leather. Like a wax doll eaten by time, Amelia Campbell Roberts stood before them dressed in soiled silks and disintegrating tulle. Her once-golden curls were frizzed and matted, bunched and tied with faded ribbon, the hairline lifting from the scalp like a cheap wig. Round patches of rouge and dead-white powder replaced the peaches and cream complexion, her rosebud mouth was carefully rouged on to withered skin. She might have been pitiful, a pathetic parody of the beautiful little girl she must once have been, if it was not for the eyes. These looked out from their grey shadowed sockets, black as buttons, void of any human emotion, blank and pitiless.

She held a fat sputtering candle up, wafting it backwards and forwards in front of their faces. Hot wax splashed and set on her hand but she did not react, or even seem to notice.

"Thank you for joining us. We so like new blood," she smiled in welcome. Her gums were black. Her teeth a row of filed metal points. "So nice to see you here," she added, in a breathy little-girl voice, lisping and horrible. "If not entirely unexpected. Come."

"What have you done with my sister?" Jake demanded. He did not know what this creature was; or how she came to be here; he just wanted Amy.

"You'll see soon enough," she said with a little laugh, a tiny silvery chuckle which sent a chill through him. "We have other guests to arrive. It is rude to start without everyone present. We have been waiting, you see. My friends and I." She clasped her hands and skipped from side to side. "I do so love parties. Surprise, surprise! It's party time!"

Her voice rang out, a shrill clarion call. What Cassie and Jake had taken to be piles and mounds of rags began to stir and move. Suddenly, the space was filled. All around, creatures began to unfold, like strange insects from mouldering chrysalises. They were child-size, but there all similarity ended. These things were more like hideous dwarves, horrible midgets, plucked from some terrible medieval vision of hell. Some were gaunt and thin, black eyes huge and wide against parchment skin. Others were grossly bloated, lumpy parodies of baby chubbiness, eyes greedy little beady gleams in leprous white pouches of fat. Still more were red and flayed-looking, blue-green veins squirming and worming across hairless skull and forehead.

The light from Jake's helmet raked across the horde of strange creatures swarming towards them. Dressed in a peculiar mixture of garments, old and new, bright and dowdy, they looked like nightmare clowns, or some weird scarecrow army. Each one the lamp found shied a little bit, but still they came on. Cassie and Jake moved instinctively, edging away, drawing back in fear and revulsion until they could retreat no further. They found themselves backed up against some kind of platform. A raised dais spread with ragged rugs and scraps of ancient carpet. Stained pillows and rotting mattresses were scattered as though for some kind of hellish picnic.

Amy was there, clothes torn and dirty, fair hair hanging in knotted tangles, her face stained and streaked with tears. She was struggling to get to her brother, but the creature squatting by her side pulled her back. She cried out to him in wordless distress, her mouth gagged with a filthy rag.

The other little girl with her looked to be in a bad way. She lay motionless, eyes closed, her pale skin tinged a violet blue. There were a number of small wounds on her arms and face. Small slits with ragged chewed-looking edges, and round red rings like the marks left by suction cups.

Cassie surged forward to reach her, fearing she might be dead already. Jake made a break at the same time, but they both found themselves instantly restrained, thin arms wove their way round them, holding them back, pinioned and helpless. They struggled, but these creatures were strong, stronger than they looked. Long black nails curved and grown into razor sharp claws gripped like vices, piercing the tough fabric of their water proof clothing, cutting through to the skin. Helmet lights went out as leads were wrenched from battery-packs. Jake's torch was snatched from his hand and smashed on the floor leaving them in darkness.

They both struggled and kicked, fighting back, the claws holding them tightening, biting in, ripping deep into their arms and legs. The more they fought, the more hands grabbed and held on to them, and still more, until Cassie felt like a modern Gulliver in some dreadful Lilliput, pinned and immobilized. She stood still, breath rasping, her whole body shaking as the warm blood seeped and ran down inside her clothes.

Behind them came a muffled scream as one of the creatures started on Amy. It was only then that Jake stopped struggling.

"That's better. You will only hurt yourselves and those you care about. You can't go yet, you see!" Amelia's lispy little voice expressed shock and surprise at the very idea. "That would be rude. Very rude indeed. And I don't like rudeness. Think of the fun we will have!" She laughed, her eerie chuckle cracked and thin. "Down here we can play for ever and ever! You and Amy and Cassie and Wendy; you all are going to join us. Be our new playmates!"

A rustle of excitement spread through the surrounding mob. Teeth as sharp as hers, metal bright in blackened mouths, glistened in anticipation.

26

There was some kind of commotion at the back of the eager crowd. A confused muttering started up, an excited gibbering. They were milling around, moving out of the way, dropping back in confusion.

Amelia turned to see what was causing the disturbance, calling out, "Who's there?"

There was an edge of doubt in her voice and Jake felt the grip on him slacken. His captors turned, trying to see through the jostling crowd, trying to work out what was going on. That was all the opportunity Jake needed. He sloughed off the restraining hands, unslung his rucksack, and aimed it at the creature guarding Amy. The heavy pack got him a good one. The creature rolled away and lay stunned and unmoving, curled up in a ball. Quick as lightning, Amy scuttled over to her brother.

"Are you all right?"

She nodded, her eyes huge, blue rings round black pupil. He pulled the gag away from her mouth.

"They said you were up Runghills, on your bike. Said you'd had an accident. That Billy kid, he did…"

"Never mind that." Jake smiled, trying to impart a calm he did not feel. "Are your hands free?"

She nodded. "They aren't all that good at knots."

"OK, in my bag, at the bottom, there's a big lamp…"

She was back in her place, small fingers working the straps, before his captors made another grab for him and pulled him back.

The darkness was not total. There was just enough light to see what had caused the commotion. It was Billy. The crowd parted to let him through. Cassie's heart leapt. Fraser was with him, walking by Billy's side, dwarfing all the others as he picked his way across the nightmare campsite.

"There she is, see?" He turned to his tall companion. "Told you she was safe." He waved a thin finger up at Fraser. "Now, no funny stuff. Or, like I said, you'll get her throat slit."

As if on cue, Cassie felt a hand as thin and hard as bone wind round her throat and a needle-sharp claw prick the skin above the jugular.

"It's cold in here." Billy's arms went round his thin body. "You won't be needing that any more." He tugged at Fraser's long coat. "Give it to me."

Fraser seemed utterly fearless as he sloughed off the coat but his breathing was bad; Cassie could hear it as he came towards her. He stood next to her, his face impassive, not looking at her, not looking at anybody, automatically patting the space where his pocket had been.

Billy draped the coat over his own shoulders. It nearly

200

swallowed his thin frame up, dragging along the floor as he came towards them. It looked heavy on him, weighted down, something clinked deep in the pockets.

"Did I do good?" He smiled down at his sister who had come to inspect her final captive.

"You did splendidly," she reached up to plant a withered kiss on his cheek, "but then you always do, Billy." She clapped her hands, turning towards the dais. "Now we can begin…"

There was a click, and a white flash.

The thick beam, powerful as a searchlight, caught Amelia full in the face. She let out a high shrieking scream and her black eyes seemed to crinkle in their sockets like burning cellophane. Amy moved forward, turning the lamp on to the creatures that held Jake and Cassie. They released their grip, cringing and curling away from the blazing light like slugs from salt. Then she turned it on the rest of them.

Skeletal arms went up, trying to ward off the blue-white sickening glare. Cries of dismay rang out as the massing creatures instinctively backed up, falling over each other in their panic to escape the brightness searing into them.

Cassie leapt on to the platform. She leaned over Wendy, putting two fingers on her throat. There was a pulse, but only just. Fraser reached past her and hoisted the little body up into his arms. Amy threw the light to Jake and indicated for Cassie and Fraser to follow her.

"This way! I've seen 'em go in and out over here!"

She dodged around a large throne affair, a moth-eaten wing-back chair perched on top of old tea chests. Behind it, and to the left, was a dark space. They made for that,

Jake coming last, walking backwards, keeping the light fully on the creatures edging forward. He sent the throne crashing as he went past, turned on his heels and ran for it.

Perhaps he was more used to the light outside, but Billy was leading the charge after them. He skipped round and over the falling chests, well ahead of the others.

The gap in the wall led into a high stone corridor. At the end was a flight of steps and at the top of these was a great wooden door. Amy reached it first, turning the big iron ring set into it, but the door wouldn't budge. Cassie tried then, tears of frustration glazing her eyes, fear making her fingers slip on the twisted metal. Still it would not move.

"Other way! Other way!" Fraser shouted from behind her. "You twist, I'll shove."

Together they made it work. The latch rose and the heavy door creaked back on rusty hinges.

"Quick! Quick! Take the kid!"

Fraser passed the little girl to Cassie and shepherded them through one at a time. The door was half a metre thick but would only open a couple of inches. Amy slipped through, then Cassie. Jake went next. The baying behind was getting bad, they were near, getting nearer.

"Come on, Fraser!"

"No. You go. Get them out of here. Out into the air. *Go!*"

Jake did as he was told, leaving Fraser to cover their retreat. Billy came on, ahead of the rest. He reached Fraser first.

"Here you are. You'll be needing this." Fraser's outstretched hand held a zippo lighter. "Good luck."

"And you. So long, Fraser."

The boy looked up with his impossibly ancient old man's eyes and smiled.

"So long, Billy."

Fraser nearly added, "Be seeing you", but he knew that wouldn't be true. He closed the door, blinking back the tears that were stinging in his nose and catching at the back of his throat. He would never see Billy again; not in this life, anyway.

The general cry of rage and fury was audible through inches of solid oak as Fraser dropped the thick bar down into place. These cries faded to nothing as he ran and ran, following the others, up and up spiral stairs, out of the old city gate and into the quiet gardens surrounding the Brideswell. The ancient circular lake had filled beyond capacity, making the ground wet and squelchy even here. Their feet sank into the grass and mud as they stood still for a moment, trying to acclimatize, trying to recover themselves. The floor water was subsiding; it was an ebbing tide, being drawn away and down through the storm drains into underground tunnels which were already raging torrents of swirling water.

"Quick, quick!" Amy plucked at Fraser's arm, her eyes huge with worry about what might be flying up the stairs after them. "We better go..."

"No," Fraser gasped out, "there's no hurry."

A series of dull detonations shook the ground under their feet. Billy had gone back into the seething mass, hands thrust deep into the pockets of the older boy's coat. He stood for a moment, as if lost in thought, and then one at a time he took out the homemade bombs he and Fraser had constructed. These were crude affairs, squat glass pop bottles filled with petrol, but effective enough. Billy lit one after another with the zippo lighter belonging to his friend and lobbed them up in the air to arc across and explode in the foul mess around him. For a fleeting second, he wished Fraser could have been there to see it, but that was impossible. Fraser had a life to live, and there was no way out from here. No escape from the inferno beginning to rage. Amelia led her brood, running like rats, this way and that, seeking for an exit, but there was no exit.

They piled up against stout oak and steel doors shut tight against them. They were pushed back from storm waters rushing past in a solid mass. One or two threw themselves in, only to be whirled and twirled away in the turbulent current and dashed to pieces, torn to shreds on spiked iron gratings erected to comb out foreign bodies. Fire and water. The flames licked towards Billy, greedy for him, too. Cleansed by fire and water. This was no place for the living. Billy began to smile.

27

The flames ate their way up from the basement, creeping along heating and ventilation ducts, roaring up lift shafts and along corridors, consuming floor after floor until the fire at the old hospital lit the night sky. It cast a red glow over the whole central part of the city, so bright that those old enough were reminded of the worst days of the Blitz.

Sirens wailed through the wet deserted streets, fire machines dashed from everywhere to try and contain the blaze. By morning it was over. The local news on breakfast TV showed firemen damping down and picking through smouldering blackened ruins. No one was hurt. No one had been in the disused building at the time, looking for a place to sleep, sheltering from the storm. The city's dossers and down and outs never used it. Even in the severest of weathers, they would risk a soaking, would freeze in doorways rather than pass a night in that particular building.

The general opinion was that the fire was a blessing in disguise. It got rid of an eyesore, saved the council the trouble.

The same news bulletin reported on the remarkable rescue of the city's two missing children from a complex of underground tunnels. A police statement described how the children must have wandered into old mine workings and become lost. Their discovery was due to the brave actions and quick thinking of experienced caver, Jake Saunders, and his friend, Cassie Johnson.

The statement was short. Extremely brief. It did not mention certain details which worried the police. The tunnels were extensive, it was easy to get lost in there, but how had the younger of the two, Wendy Richardson, survived for so long underground? And how was it that she and Amy Saunders had emerged miles away from the suspected place of entry?

They would probably never know the answers to these questions. The younger child, although expected to make a full recovery, was still in intensive care. She was unlikely to remember much of her ordeal and her parents had already issued instructions that she was not to be questioned about it. She was safe and, as far as they were concerned, that was the end of it. Amy Saunders just said she got lost and then her brother, Jake, had come and found her. The police and medical staff were also puzzled by the exact nature of the wounds found on Wendy's body. The final diagnosis was animal bites, most probably from rats. After all, what other explanation could there be?

The police questioned Cassie, Fraser and Jake but they could throw no light on the odder aspects of the case. When asked about their own cuts and scratches, they replied they had done them on rocks, iron spikes, and scrap left underground. They were cleaned up in Casualty and allowed to go home.

Cassie and Fraser left the hospital together. Amy was being kept in overnight, just to make sure she was all right, and Jake was staying with her. The other two offered to keep him company, but he told them to go on home, he'd be OK.

They all stood together under the canopy outside the hospital entrance, linked by their shared experience, reluctant to leave each other.

Jake looked out at the still-falling rain and back at the two of them.

"Thanks…" he began to say.

"What for?" Fraser asked, genuinely puzzled.

"For being there for me. Helping to look for Amy. You risked your lives, and you didn't have to do it…"

"Don't be stupid." Cassie hugged him to her. "What are friends for, right?"

"Yeah, don't even think about it." Fraser grinned and shook Jake's hand. "You go back and look after your little sister. I'll see you Wednesday."

"Wednesday?" Cassie asked as they walked down the drive together. "What's happening on Wednesday?"

"Oh, there's a meeting of the Climbing Club. They've got a trip planned for the holidays. Jake asked if I was up for it."

"Climbing?"

"Yeah. What's wrong with that?"

"Nothing."

She looked at him. He was dishevelled, dirty, his T-shirt was filthy, his jeans torn at the knees. He looked exhausted, he needed a shave and the rest of his face was grey under the sodium street lights but, apart from all that, he looked relaxed, at ease with himself. The trouble had gone from his eyes; for the first time since she had known him, Fraser looked happy.

"What are you looking at?"

"Nothing. You."

"Great story, eh?" he said, putting his arm round her. "Not just for *Orbit* – with any luck the nationals might pick it up…"

"Oh, hey! No." Cassie shook her head. "We stick strictly to facts from now on. No more 'Anything Weird Will Do', no more 'Stranger than Fiction'…"

Fraser laughed, "I was only kidding. After all – who'd believe it?" He looked down at her. "You're right, no more Psi Files." He smiled, green eyes glinting. "Not for a while, anyway."

Andy promised to come back later that evening. He could see that going out was not an option. However much Ellen was pretending, it was clear how ill she was. So he promised to bring along some home entertainment.

He arrived about eight o'clock, armed with videos and a large carrier bag.

"I've got popcorn, two sorts. A couple of bottles of Coke and ice-cream for the interval. I didn't know what kind you liked, so I got one plain and one with nuts and bits. Is that all right?"

He looked so concerned, Ellen laughed out loud and he grinned back. Her laughter was so rare these days it sounded odd even to her own ears. It was such a relief to be with someone who wasn't always serious.

"What films did you get?"

"'Interview with a Vampire' and 'Dracula'. Kind of deep background."

Ellen's grandmother shuddered. "I don't know how you young people can watch such things." She stood up. "I'll leave you to it. Give me the ice-cream. It had better go in the freezer before it melts everywhere. I'll say good-night. I have a couple of letters to write and then I'm going to bed."

"Night, Gran."

"Good-night, Mrs Baxter."

"Ellen isn't well, remember," she said, turning to Andy. "Don't keep her up too late."

"No, I won't. I promise. I've read the diary," he said to Ellen after her grandmother left the room.

"What do you think?"

"I'd like to see the next one – when you finish it. It seems unbelievable – but when you think about what it says in that…" He indicated the file of newspaper cuttings which lay on the table. "If you put the two together…"

"Exactly." Ellen leaned forward. There was something she wanted to discuss with him. "You don't think it could happen now, do you? I mean, I've been reading this stuff – and being this close to the cemetery – it's beginning to give me the creeps."

"The diaries – that all happened a long time ago –" Andy put his hand on her shoulder, trying to reassure her – "the modern sightings were all outside, at night. You aren't going to go wandering around there after dark, are you?"

"What if they can get in? There was a girl. Look…"

She opened the folder to a picture taken from the local

gazette. The girl had long hair, parted in the middle, sixties style. She was sitting on a bed, eyes fixed on the camera, a crucifix held out in front of her.

The headline read: *Vampire Girl Tells Of Terror Ordeal*.

Ellen shivered. She'd read the story. She had read all of them several times and now she wished she had never asked to see his collection of clippings. The diaries were one thing; even if they were true she was separated from the events by more than a century. The newspaper stories made it much more real. Closer to home – literally.

"Let's face it," she added, leafing through, "they don't exactly have far to go."

Andy shook his head. "They have to be invited in. Vampires can't cross a threshold unless they are invited."

"How do you know?"

"I read it somewhere. Or maybe I saw it, in one of these movies. I know it's scary, but you mustn't let your imagination get the upper hand. Are you sure you want to see these? If you feel nervous about it, we could watch something else."

"Like what? You've brought them now. We might as well take a look."

The films had lost their power to frighten her. They were so obviously fictional, obviously unreal, that Ellen even felt soothed by them. She leaned back against Andy and it seemed only natural for him to put his arm round her as they shared a bowl of popcorn, and then for her to rest her head against his chest to watch the movie. She could relax into him, feel his heart beating. His presence was comforting. She was glad she'd shared the diaries with him.

Ellen was nearly asleep as the first film ended and Andy announced the interval. He went to get the ice-cream and they shared a second bottle of Coke. Ellen spooned up pralines 'n' cream and settled back to watch the trailers. Suddenly something cold slid down the front of her shirt.

"Hey! What are you doing?"

"That's what you do with this kind of ice-cream. You put it down people's shirts, I've seen it on the adverts. Didn't you know?"

"Right!" Ellen loaded her scoop and turned on him.

"Ellen! No!"

Edith Baxter smiled to herself as she heard the whoops and shrieks coming from downstairs. It was so good to hear Ellen laugh again. Stella would probably not approve, but she knew in her heart it would do no harm. Whatever ailed the girl, it was wrong to keep her away from the normal world. She must be allowed the freedom to behave like any other teenager.

"It's late." Andy pressed the remote to rewind the video and gently shifted Ellen's sleeping weight from his arm. "Ellen?" He pushed away the strands of hair that had fallen across her face. "Wake up. I have to go."

She opened her eyes, bewildered for a moment, and looked up into his. He was close, so close his image was blurring. Then her mouth met his. The video rewound itself and clicked off. A TV programme started up and went unnoticed. Eventually it was Andy who broke away. He opened his eyes wide, like he was waking up, and smiled.

"Hey," he said, "I really have to go…"

He stood up and went to retrieve his videos.

"Whatever I've got, it's not catching, you know," Ellen said as she handed him his coat.

"It's not that. It's just, if your gran comes down and finds me still here, I'll be banned for life and never be able to see you again…"

"Do you want to?"

He put his arms round her and kissed her again, light and quick.

"What do you think? Now I really must go." He zipped up his jacket. "I've got to be up bright and early."

"When will I see you? Tomorrow?"

"Not tomorrow. I'm going on a trip. Won't be back till late. Day after?"

"Promise?"

The central heating must have gone off, Ellen was beginning to shiver.

"Good-night."

"Night, Andy."

She went to see him out. A leaf blew in over the threshold. "Unless invited in…" Ellen knew it was silly, but she trapped it with her foot and edged it back on to the top step before shutting the door.

Andy went down the path. Even as the door closed, he wanted to see her again, talk to her. He had never felt like this about a girl. It was like he was only half in the real world. He had caught something all right, and whatever it was could be terminal. He was thinking this, and smiling to himself, as he rounded the corner where the short drive met the road. He turned sharply right and walked straight into someone.

Andy felt the shock, and registered the impact, with a swift intake of breath.

"I didn't see you. Sorry."

"Don't apologize. It was entirely my fault. Are you OK?" A gloved hand steadied his arm. "You seem shaken."

The deep voice sounded American, laced with a trace of some other accent.

"No, I'm fine," Andy replied. "I just wasn't expecting…"

He must have just been standing there, in the shadow of the tall hedge. There had been no sound, no warning footsteps. Andy looked up but could see little of his face under the wide fedora.

"If you are sure…" Teeth showed white, shining in the street light. "I'll bid you good-night."

The man touched the brim of his hat and walked away. The pavement glistened, frost lay thick; it might even have been snowing a little bit. The man's heels rang loud in the silence of the empty street. When he reached the corner, he glanced back for a second, and then he was gone. Andy looked down. He could see no footsteps in the whiteness on the ground.

Like many older people, Edith Baxter was a light sleeper. She had no idea what it was, but something caused her to wake in the early hours of the morning. She groped for her glasses and sat up in bed, listening for any noise from inside the house.

She could hear nothing, but still she got out of bed and found her robe. There was still no sound, just the distant ticking of the hall clock. She padded down the corridor towards the door of the room where Ellen slept.

There was no noise, no sound. The creature on the bed

laboured silently, pulling itself by long spiked thumbs over the tumbled bedclothes. Dark leathery wings lay on its back, fine membranes folded round fingers, fantastically elongated, but as finely articulated as those on a human hand. Small eyes glowed red like tiny coals as it crept away from the sleeper's arm resting on the counterpane. A tiny slit showed on the white underside, just above the place where the veins snaked up from the wrist in fine blue tracery. This was the area the bat had chosen, slashing through the skin with incisors as sharp as razors, grooved tongue lapping the blood, the flow maintained by a powerful anticoagulant. It stopped crawling now, having sensed a disturbance. Not in this room, but somewhere in the house.

Edith Baxter opened the door and sensed nothing at all. Except that it was cold. She hugged her dressing gown to her and went over to the window. It was only open a crack, but that was enough. On a night like this, the girl could catch her death. She pulled it shut, securing the lock on the top. Just at that moment, she looked up. Something black spiralled up, whirled like a leaf between her and the street light, and was gone. The movement, odd and erratic, reminded her of bats. There were plenty of roosts over in the cemetery, but she had to be mistaken. Bats hibernate in the wintertime, surely? More likely to be dirt on her glasses. She took them off and examined the lenses. Hopelessly smeary, polishing just made them worse.

Edith Baxter tucked her granddaughter's arm back in and straightened the counterpane. In the darkness, she failed to notice the slight cut, the tiny drops of blood. The girl's hair was damp, skin slightly feverish to the touch.

She moaned slightly, and her head turned on the pillow. Her eyes tracked rapidly, scanning beneath the lids, but she did not wake. She was far removed in time and place, deep in a dream in which she had become the other Ellen.